Dark

&

Bitter

Short

Stories

By

Authors from 518 & Yonder

Text copyright © 2017 by 518 Publishing Company LLC

Cover copyright © 2017 by Jaz Johnson

ISBN-13: 978-1979073486
ISBN-10: 1979073481

Author Signature Page

Rachael Crawford - _____

Rosanne Braslow - _____

SJ Garman - _____

Sam T. Willis - _____

Andy Lee - _Andy Lee_ Thank you.

Sandy Brewster - _Sandy - Thank you for the support! Sandy Brewster_

Jaz Johnson - _____

Shannon Yseult - _____

Shan Jeniah Burton - _Shan Jeniah Burton_

Brian Black - _____

Lizette Strait - _____

Special Acknowledgement to Kickstarter. Without the crowd funder, this book would not be possible. Also a shout out to our top supporters.

Wompa - Without whom this book would not have been thought of.

All the Lees - Who were kind enough to support us through all of our troubles.

Geoff & Dawn Harvey - Full of support and love for our new found venture.

Mary Beth Frezon - A wonderful friend, who has been there since the beginning.

Allyson Werner & Lucas Werner - Who helped us in a time of need.

Evelyn Kauderer - Without whom our writing community would not have existed.

TABLE
OF
CONTENTS

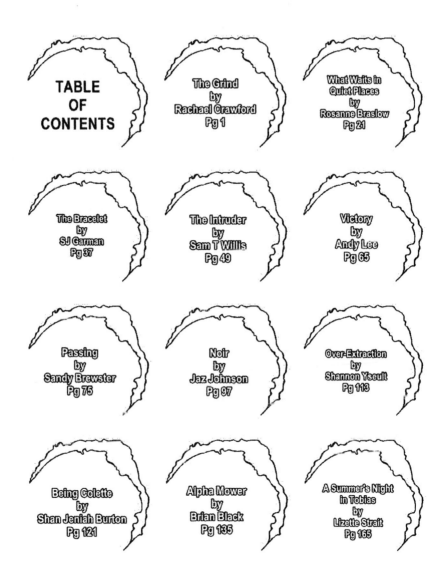

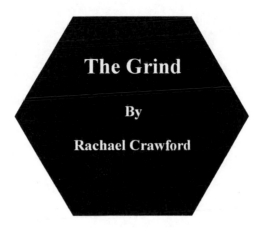

The Grind

By

Rachael Crawford

"Ugh, this dance is exhausting," said Miranda Winters, slumping down next her best friend, Olivia James.

"It looks it," responded Olivia, glad for once that she couldn't sing very well and so had decided to act as stage manager for the spring musical.

"I only have five minutes," said Miranda in between big gulps of water, "What up?"

"Nothing new since you saw me in English."

"Oh really? I thought you sat next to Joey in math," Miranda teased.

"Nothing, I swear," Olivia said, blushing. Miranda always knew just how tease her. Not that it mattered. They had been best friends their whole lives, so the teasing was nothing new.

"Ok, break over. Places," called a voice from the stage. The choreographer, a college student named Melissa, was standing with her hands on her hips.

Miranda, who was the dance captain, rose, said a quick goodbye, and jumped up to join Melissa. Even though she played the female lead and wasn't in this number she still needed to learn it, so she could help the others.

Olivia watched her friend go and then turned back to the papers in front of her. As stage manager one of her major responsibilities was figuring out the rehearsal schedule. Since a lot of the kids in the show had other clubs and sports, it was not easy to figure out which scenes and dances they could rehearse on which day. Today was Thursday, she needed to get next week's schedule up by tomorrow morning so everyone could make plans over the weekend. Mrs.

Hall, her English teacher and director, wanted to rehearse the party scene and the song "Cross the Line" next week. The problem was that nearly everyone in the cast was in that scene. Finding a day that everyone could actually come was nearly impossible.

"What do you mean no one can leave?" came a familiar voice from behind her.

Olivia turned around to see two shadowy figures standing in the back of the theatre. She recognized the first one as Mrs. Hall. The other figure was harder to discern. Olivia strained her neck, trying to see them. While it wasn't unusual for Mrs. Hall to pop her head in during dance rehearsals, she rarely said anything, let alone something loud enough for Olivia to hear.

Unfortunately all she could hear was Joey, her crush, and Nancy, the sophomore girl playing Miss. Watson. Nancy was having a hard time getting the timing right on her part. Olivia felt bad for Nancy. This song was really her only chance to shine, and it was not easy. It was a fast number, and timing was critical, as a lot of different people were coming in and out of the scene. Still, she clearly had a long way to go, and her screw ups were making it awfully hard to hear what Mrs. Hall and the mysterious man were saying.

Getting up and moving closer was the easiest way to eavesdrop, Olivia decided. But she couldn't make it obvious. Slowly, she stood up and moved toward the back of the auditorium, making it look like she was checking sight lines along the way. After a minute or two she settled herself into the back row, directly in front of the whispering adults.

She still couldn't make out the man's face. From where she sat, he simply looked dark and bitter. Olivia pretended to go back to her scheduling, hoping she could hear them.

"I can't tell these kids not to leave. For one, their parents would kill me," Olivia could barely make out Mrs. Hall's voice.

"I'm sorry. But until we find out who did this, no one can leave," said the man.

"Well, can't we just ask them?"

"I'm afraid not. The police don't want to spook anyone."

"Well then, Mr. Koonce, you will just have to explain to all these parents why their children can't go home, on a school night."

So it was Mr. Koonce, the principal. That made sense. And the police were looking for something. But what or maybe who were they looking for? Olivia certainly didn't want to be stuck here any longer than necessary. She loved rehearsal and all, but she had a ton of homework to do for tomorrow, and she liked her sleep.

"Mrs. Hall, you have an hour left here right? Surely the test will be found by then. In the meantime, please don't tell anyone about this."

"Fine," Mrs. Hall sighed.

Olivia slunk down in her chair as the two parted ways. So a test had been stolen. It must be an important one too if the police had been called. Then Olivia remembered her mother, who taught history, saying something about the state tests arriving early. That must be it. Some kid must have taken one of them. Olivia knew from the stupid thing they always made her sign that having previous knowledge of the test was a big no-no.

As stupid as this was, Olivia did not want to be stuck here any longer, she could practically hear her stomach grumbling and knew her mom had dinner waiting at home. Since apparently the police weren't going to do much, at least not here, Olivia would have to figure it out for herself.

Her first thought was to just look in the backpacks of all the kids, but she knew they would see her and cause an uproar. No, she would have to find some other way. She looked up on stage at the kids rehearsing "Coffee Black." The first thing to do would be to figure out who had motive.

Flipping to the list of people who had to be here today, she began noting who was taking the tests. It was January, which meant that very few people cared about Regents. Most people took them in June. All the freshman could be eliminated, none of them had finished enough classes to take an exam once, let alone need to retake it. She knew for a fact that no one in her class had failed anything last year, which cut out the juniors. That left the sophomores and seniors.

The seniors were the most likely. If they wanted to graduate in June this was one of their last chances to pass. Still, she couldn't eliminate the sophomores entirely. All in all she was left with ten suspects. If only she had access to grades.

That reminded her that surely the cops had access to grades, meaning that angle was already being looked at. Being a cop's daughter, she knew a decent amount about procedure, and actually, her father was probably the one investigating. They would have checked which kids needed to pass this test first thing. Since they still didn't know who it was, more than one person must have failed.

Olivia was so involved in her thoughts that she didn't even notice that the music had stopped until Miranda spoke.

"Whatcha doing?"

"Huh, oh nothing?"

"Why'd you cross me off the list? I thought I had to be here every day?"

"Oh, you do. I'm doing, something else."

"Still doesn't explain why I'm crossed off. I thought I was your best friend."

"You are, don't worry. Listen," Olivia changed the subject, "is anyone acting strange up there?"

"No stranger than usual. Why?"

"No reason. No one's nervous about anything?"

"Nope. What's going on, Liv?"

"Nothing. Why aren't you onstage anyway?" asked Olivia, finally realizing how strange it was that rehearsal had stopped.

"Oh, Melissa had to take a call. So she told us all to work on our homework, like anyone's gonna do that."

She was right, of course. All around the auditorium small groups of friends where talking. Not a single kid had their book out. Olivia had hoped she could find people who were studying, though someone who stole a test wouldn't exactly need to study. She decided she could work on this when rehearsal started again and instead enjoy these few minutes with her friend.

It wasn't long before Miranda and the others were back onstage, singing about how much they loved coffee.

The first thing Olivia needed to do was find a suspect. All the singing and dancing would provide a great cover. But how could she even figure out who was taking a test? The schedule.

Rehearsals during regents' week, she had asked everyone for a list of tests they were taking.

Olivia rifled through the papers she had with her, but she couldn't find the list. What if she had left it at home? Then she remembered working on the schedule during history. Ok, so she knew she should have been paying attention in class. But when your mom is a history teacher, though luckily not her history teacher, you kind of already know the subject pretty well.

She jumped up and went to get her book bag. Digging through her various notebooks and folders, not to mention the other assorted crap she searched for the Regents list. *I really should clean this out.* Finally she found it, wedged in between her history notebook and a quiz they'd gotten back.

Olivia took it out and smoothed down the wrinkles. As she remembered, it was a pretty short list. In fact, there were only two tests being taken by four students. That certainly narrowed down the suspect list. Hank Lewis, Ben Vindow, and Gretchen Gardner were taking American History on Tuesday morning. Then, Ben and Joey Cavanaugh were taking Course Two Math on Thursday.

She was surprised to see Joey's name on the list for the math test. After all, he was in her course three class. Why would they have let him take the next level of math if he had failed the test? She definitely needed to talk to him.

That thought made her stomach flutter a little. Ugh, yes she had a little crush, but there was no way he felt the same way. Joey barely ever talked to her, unless he needed something for the show. Still, the opportunity to strike up a conversation sounded sweet! Hopefully, he wasn't guilty, because that would certainly put a damper on her hopes for a prom date.

A glance at the rest of the list reminded Olivia that she should remove one more suspect. Hank wasn't at rehearsal that day. He had been out all week because his Uncle had died. It was all very sad, and it definitely took him out of the pool of suspects.

That left three possibilities: Ben, Joey, and Gretchen. If only she knew which test had been stolen, it would make things easier. She looked quickly up at the stage. Only Joey was up there now, with Melissa and Miranda. They were going over some of his more difficult choreography.

The rest of the cast was supposed to be going over other things on their own, but Olivia could see that most of them had split into smaller groups and were just chatting. She spied Ben in a corner by himself. Though it was odd to see him alone, it gave Olivia just the chance she needed.

"Hey, Ben," she said, pulling up next to him.

"Oh, Liv, hi," he said, jumping a little in his seat, "Do you need something?"

It was unusual for her to talk to him, since they weren't exactly friends, and they didn't have any classes together, either.

"Um," Olivia stalled, trying to think of something to say. "I, uh, I noticed you're taking two tests next week," she jumped right to the punch.

"Yeah, but I already told you that."

"Right, um . . . Mrs. Hall . . . she wanted to make sure you didn't need more days off from rehearsal for review."

"Oh, thanks, I guess. But no, I'm good. That's actually what I'm doing now," he patted the book in his hand, "I know I bombed these tests back in June, but I'm pretty confident this time."

He went back to reading his review book, so Olivia took the hint and walked away. *Was he so confident because he had the test answers? If he had the answers, why did he need to keep studying? Was it just a ruse to keep people from catching him? But who would he be hiding from? No one else here even knew the test was missing.* She thought this was all just way too confusing.

Just as she was about to sit down and think over her whole plan, the mystery came to her in the form of Gretchen Gardner.

"Liv, hey. I'm supposed to talk to you about schedule changes, right?" said the girl breathlessly.

"Hm, oh yeah," answered Olivia, a bit flustered.

"Well, I know I said I had a test next week but I don't anymore."

"Oh really? Why?"

"Well, turns out I don't need to take it after all. I mean, I passed in June, but not by a lot. My stupid parents wanted me to take it again, but we had a meeting with guidance today and they're convinced it's all cool."

"Oh, that's great. So you're available all next week then?"

"Yup," she said, flouncing back to her friends.

One more suspect off her list. She was down to just Ben and Joey. As she walked over to her seat, she tried to come up with a way for it to just be Ben.

Then this could be over and she didn't have to embarrass herself with Joey. But she just couldn't eliminate either boy as a suspect. She only had one choice.

A few moments later, Melissa called everyone back onstage. This time she wanted Joey to sit so the rest of the dancers could go over their bit. They were dancing with coffee cups and it needed to be perfected so they didn't drop any. Olivia was glad to hear this, because she did not need an audience for this discussion.

Joey took his seat in the auditorium and pulled out a book. Olivia took a deep breath, looked up at the stage to make sure no one was watching, and strode over to him.

"Hey," she said, sitting down next to him.

"Oh, hi Liv," said Joey, looking surprised to see her, "What's up?"

Just as she was about to answer, a lock of his gorgeous brown hair fell in front of eye. Her breath caught in her throat, *Wow, he was handsome.*

"Liv?" he asked, and she realized she was staring.

"Oh, sorry, right. Um, I just wanted to talk to

you about the schedule for next week," she decided to use the same lie she had with Ben. "Mrs. Hall just wanted to check and see if you were attending any review classes."

"Oh, um, nah, I don't think so. I mean, I'm still taking the class, so I think I'm good."

"But you're in my math class," Olivia said without thinking.

"I've got two actually. It was the only way to stay on track to graduate."

"I didn't know they let you do that."

"They don't usually, but my dad can be a bit of a hard ass, and he talked them into it."

"Oh, um, good for you."

"Thanks. The good news is they said if I do well enough, I can drop the other class."

"Cool."

"Yeah, of course, if I fail again, my dad might kill me."

"I hope he doesn't," Olivia said with a giggle. It was a sound she had never heard come out of her mouth before and she regretted instantly. Luckily, he laughed too. "Well, I better go. Good luck."

"Thanks."

She walked back to her seat, almost afraid to look back in his direction. When she finally did, his head was back in his book, and she wasn't sure if that was a good thing. Unfortunately, her suspect list didn't look so good. Neither boy could be crossed off, but neither was a good suspect. Both were typically good kids, not exactly the type to steal a test. But Principal Koonce would have let them leave if he didn't think there was some chance someone here had done it.

Joey went back onstage, leaving Olivia as the only one in the audience. She sat silently for a while, trying to figure out what to do next. Then she heard the door to the auditorium open behind her.

Olivia swiveled around and saw two figures in the doorway. The first, unsurprisingly, was Mrs. Hall. Olivia had figured she would be back soon. The second gave Olivia mixed feelings. While she was always happy to see him, the sight of her dad, Robert James, in uniform at her school, was not a good sign. He could only be here because of the theft.

He saw her, too, and motioned for her to join them. Olivia rose and went to the back door.

"Daddy? Why are you here?" Olivia asked,

trying to mask the fact that she already knew the answer.

"Work business, Livvy Bear."

"Uh Oh."

"Liv, your dad needs to know who is taking a test next week. You have that information, don't you?" asked Mrs. Hall.

"Um, yeah, let me go grab it."

She went to get the paper. Luckily she had written her notes on a separate sheet. On her way, Miranda glanced at her from the stage and gave Olivia a look. Olivia shrugged, grabbed the paper, and went back to the adults.

"Here," she said, handing the list to her dad, then, remembering, "Oh, but Gretchen isn't taking it anymore. She just told me a few minutes ago."

"Thanks, Livvy Bear, see you at home," her dad said.

She went back to her seat, half disappointed that she hadn't solved anything, half glad that she didn't have to deal with it anymore. The group onstage took a break, but Olivia stayed in her place. Miranda was busy with one of the girls who was confused about the dance, but she made it clear from her look that she wanted to talk later.

Olivia wasn't surprised to see her father go talk to Ben. After all, he was taking both tests. Though she was still interested, she looked away. All this investigating meant she hadn't done any of the scheduling work she was supposed to do. Rehearsal was going to be done soon, and she really needed to finish.

Five minutes later she was done and most of the cast was back onstage. Now all Olivia needed to do was make a copy and post it on the board outside the auditorium. She got up and, on her way out, saw her dad talking to Joey. She sighed, so much for her crush. While she hadn't had a lot of hope before, being interrogated by her father wasn't going to help the situation.

Olivia stepped into the hallway and made her way to the teacher's lounge. While students weren't usually allowed in, Mrs. Hall had made a deal that Olivia could go in once a week to copy the schedule. The room was empty. It was late in the afternoon, most of the teachers had already gone home. Olivia was glad because she hated doing this when there were teachers in the room. She always felt like she was intruding.

She made the copy and walked back to the auditorium. She pulled the thumb tack out of the current schedule and replaced it with the new one. Suddenly, she heard the door open behind her.

"What did you tell them, Liv?" asked an angry but familiar voice.

"Tell who?" she asked, turning around to find Joey standing in front of her.

"You know who. Why was your dad here? Asking those questions?"

"What questions?"

"Don't play dumb," he said, reaching out and pinning her against the wall.

Olivia had dreamed of being this close to him, but this way, she was terrified.

"I don't know what you're talking about," she said, her voice getting louder. She hoped someone would hear her and come to her rescue.

"You know exactly what I mean. You told them. About how I suck at math. And what I said about my dad."

Olivia opened her mouth to scream, but Joey covered it with his hand.

"He was going to send me to military school. I couldn't have that. So yeah, I did it, I took that stupid test. Who even cares? It's not like I'm ever going to use that crap again. But you had to run and tell daddy. Well, let's see what daddy will say now." He lifted her up off the ground and Olivia began to shake.

"Put her down," said a deep voice. Olivia saw a big hand on Joey's shoulder.

He did as he was told and stepped aside, revealing Olivia's father behind him.

"We heard the whole thing, young man."

He passed Joey off to another cop, who handcuffed him and began reading him his rights. Then he turned to Olivia.

"You okay, Livvy Bear? When I saw you were gone, and so was that boy . . ."

"I'm fine, Daddy. Just a little shaken up."

"Thank god," he turned to follow his partner, "And, Livvy,"

"Yeah?"

"Don't ever do anything that stupid again."

Dark and Bitter

What Waits in Quiet Places

By

Rosanne Braslow

Lindy stirred the ice-flecked surface of a Gibson with her index finger. She withdrew a tiny sour onion, bit down and followed it with the first silver swallow of gin. On sharp-shadowed nights like this, she was reminded of dreadful things that fester below the surface of quiet places like Catskill. It was this fear that turned her into an expert on the correct proportion of vermouth to a cocktail pitcher.

"Your better half's stuck at the courthouse."

Her father's voice startled her. He scraped a patio chair along the bluestone and settled next to her in companionable silence. The stillness of the evening was punctuated by the occasional passing car.

Carson Connor and his daughter shared the same law firm and the same lithe, handsome looks. They moved through life on long legs and had a habit of crossing them at the same easy angles. In the courtroom, they interrogated from the same cross-armed stance.

"Martini, Dad?" she asked.

Her senior partner raised a mug from which a curve of steam rose. "I've briefs to review," he said. "This cup of dark and bitter'll do me."

The autumn wind carried the scent of coffee and wood smoke. Lindy snugged a cashmere shawl around her shoulders.

"When the crickets stop, winter starts," Carson said, and whisked the zipper on his leather jacket. The dim light from the candles grew fidgety in the breeze.

That's what you said on that strange night, too, she thought.

"Wouldn't be surprised to see snow soon," he said, the mug at his lips. The steam from his cup mingled with a cloud of breath as his words rose and evaporated.

But it was still late summer, then, and I was sixteen.

She drained her glass with an eye to the far corner of the garden where the hedge was irregular with a v-shaped defect, ever since that night. More than twenty years had passed, but she remembered like it was yesterday. It began with Stuart Werner crashing through the boxwood hedges of her back yard. She'd been sitting on the same patio, and sprang from perhaps the same chair. It was mid-September. At football practice that same afternoon, Stuart had waved to her as she passed the field after class.

"Help!"

Stuart fell to his knees, breathless. His jeans and t-shirt were torn and grimy. Leafy bits of shrub stuck in his curls; scratches crisscrossed his cheeks and forehead. He gripped the sleeves of her white blouse with black fingernails, as she helped him to his feet. Her sneakers and now her arms were damp with grass clippings.

"Hide me!"

There was no one else in view.

"Come inside," she said. "You're shivering."

Murgatroyd hissed and jumped from the back steps, as Lindy led Stuart into the house.

"What's this?" Her great-aunt Ada turned from the stove as Lindy led the disheveled boy through the back door to the kitchen table. The two women exchanged an uneasy look over a pie that cooled on the counter. The house smelled of apples and cinnamon.

"Turn off the lights," Stuart said. "He'll see us!"

Lindy pressed the switch, folding the kitchen in twilight. The flame below the teakettle threw a jittery shadow. She looked out onto the empty back lawn, and without being sure why, she drew the curtains, and locked the door. A bare rectangle of window floated below the ruffled valence.

"*Who* will see us, Stuart?" Lindy's question hung for a moment in the still kitchen.

The wall phone was at her shoulder, and her hand picked up the receiver, but she let it fall back onto the hook. Her father was working late to prepare a client for trial. His office was close to home. They could call him or even the police, though she didn't know what, or even *if*, there was something to tell.

"Stuart, who's after you?" Aunt Ada asked the quivering boy. Cool light from the refrigerator spilled into the room when she reached for the milk.

"Robbie," Stuart said.

"Robbie?" Lindy and her aunt asked at the same time.

Aunt Ada poured tea for Lindy and the boy, and instant coffee for herself.

Robbie was Lindy's neighbor. And Stuart's best friend.

Why this is just a dust-up between two boys that's gotten out of hand, Lindy thought. Her shoulders relaxed, while she sipped her tea. Why she'd known Robbie her whole life.

"I'll tell you my story, but you won't believe me," Stuart said. "After football practice, Robbie and me, we drove to the old Schroeder place." There was a pause before he added, "to smoke."

"You boys shouldn't be smoking," Aunt Ada said.

Lindy wanted to tell her aunt that was beside

the point, but she didn't want to be disrespectful. As his story unwound, however, she wondered exactly what the boys had been smoking.

"We poked around the foundation of the farmhouse some," Stuart said. "For kicks. Robbie saw a piece of sheet metal he wanted. There was junk piled over it, and as we pulled it away, we found a door. To a root cellar, you know? Funny, though- it was padlocked. So, we figured it might be worth checking it out."

Lindy nodded. She would have been curious herself, though not enough to break in, mind you.

"That root cellar was deeper than we expected. It was lined with baskets full of dried-up something or other. I didn't stick my hand in to find out what. Sweet-smelling stuff.

"Smack in the middle of the floor was a long depression with a cross laid on it. Creepy, like a grave," Stuart said. "I said, *dude, let's get the hell out of here*." He turned to Aunt Ada, "Sorry, m'am.

Now, I didn't know Robbie took the cross. When I saw it I said, *dude, have some respect*, but he just tossed it into the woods."

"I was halfway in the car, and when I heard a

thud. Robbie was just a few steps from the root cellar door when he fell forward, *hard*, belly-flopping like something pulled his feet right out from under him. Man, I could feel it myself, he came down so hard."

Stuart rested his forehead on the back of his arms for a few seconds, then stared at the wall as he continued. "Robbie was dragged face-down into the root cellar, he was clawing the ground. He didn't even have time to yell, he was gone that quick. There was nothing I could do."

Aunt Ada crossed herself and pushed her glasses up her nose.

A pounding erupted at the back door.

"Lindy!" Robbie pressed his forehead and one palm to the glass as his other hand rattled the door.

Stuart jumped, knocking his chair back. He pulled Lindy and Ada, who hung onto her cup, coffee sloshing, into the dining room. They were out of Robbie's sight for a moment, before he appeared outside the tall French doors that led onto the patio.

"Lindy!" Robbie pushed and pulled on the knobs. His shoulder butted the door in an attempt to force it open.

Lindy led them up the stairs. Aunt Ada held

her cup as high she bounded upward. Robbie yelled something but she could only make out Stuart's name, as the banging and rattling moved to the front door. They huddled on the landing, out of sight.

"Robbie had the car keys," Stuart whispered. "I ran all the way into town, to the diner for help. When I got there, Robbie's car was parked in the lot, and I found him at the counter with a milkshake. Like nothing happened. But I could see. I could see something was different about him. His eyes. They looked funny. You couldn't see the blue part- it was like they were all pupil. Black holes- like you could fall right into them."

Lindy shook her head. "That doesn't make sense. What did he say?"

"He said I was crazy. That he hadn't seen me since football practice."

"But…"

"I took off. He followed me home. Tried to pull me into his car. Told me he was taking me back to the root cellar. There was a surprise waiting for me. We wrestled. He chased me through the neighborhood. That's not our friend outside, Lindy. Something *bad* is in that root cellar. It's got into

Robbie and now it wants me."

Glass shattered below.

"Come on." Lindy hurried the two into the pink and black tiled bathroom off the landing.

Just as the bathroom lock clicked into place, Lindy felt the door shudder with the impact of a body.

"Don't believe him," Robbie yelled through the door. "Open up!"

Stuart's story, crazy as it sounded, rang true. Robbie was freaking her out.

"When's Dad getting home?" she asked Aunt Ada, her voice low.

"Late, maybe ten." Her great-aunt wiped the apron across her brow and took a shaky sip of coffee.

Across the room near the sink, was a tall window with a broad sill. Lindy moved a plant and raised the window. With creative choreography, she could descend the trellis to the lawn and run for help.

"Wait," Stuart's whisper was frantic. "Don't go outside. He'll be on you in a flash. You haven't seen what he can do since... since..."

Lindy struggled to come up with another plan. At least Robbie had stopped manhandling the door. It was easier to think without all the banging and rattling.

"I'm dizzy," Stuart sat on the edge of the tub. His eyes were shadowed below dark brows, his face ivory. Lindy's first aid training told her he might be going into shock. He needed to stay warm and lie with his feet elevated. She padded the bottom of the tub with a bath towel.

"Get in," she said. He didn't argue. Aunt Ada emptied the linen closet, and they layered more towels over him. His hands were like ice as Lindy settled him with his legs up the wall.

"Let me check your pulse."

He pulled his wrist from Lindy's searching fingers. It was the first time she noticed that his fingernails weren't just dirty, they were bloodied and torn. His thumbnail lifted at what looked like a painful angle. Lindy grew uneasy recalling his story about Robbie being dragged face-down into the root cellar.

There was no longer any sound from the wild Robbie. She laid her ear against the door, listening for movement, but all seemed quiet inside the house.

Through the open window, cricket-song filled

the bathroom with a normalcy that she couldn't reconcile with Stuart laid out in her bathtub.

Aunt Ada joined Lindy, and she, too, pressed an ear to the door, the women held eye contact. "I think he's gone," Ada said.

"You're in danger," Stuart's voice echoed from inside the tub.

"Let's think." Lindy said. She crossed in front of the tub and settled on the radiator. Aunt Ada took a seat on the plush toilet seat cover, across from the sink. Lindy sank into the quiet of the house, trying to redraft Stuart's story into a plot that made sense. In the midst of the stillness, there was a voice, no *voices*, coming up the stairs.

Aunt Ada put her finger up to her lips, and a hand to Lindy's shoulder. "Someone's coming," she whispered.

"Lindy!" Her father called through the door.

"It's a trick," Stuart's voice was reed-thin. "Don't open the door."

"Carson's not supposed to be home until late," her great-aunt whispered.

Lindy bolted to the door, Aunt Ada jumped up behind her and stopped Lindy from turning the lock.

"Lindy, open the door." It was her father, calm and firm. "Robbie called me. You're in danger."

"Robbie called?" Lindy said.

"This is Sergeant Williams, Lindy." Through the door, she could make out the police dispatcher's muted chatter on his walkie-talkie. "We need to talk to Stuart."

Lindy unlocked the door and eased it open, Aunt Ada at her back. Keeping her shoulder firmly against it, she peered out. When she saw her father's face framed in the crack, she threw open the door.

"Where's Stuart?" he asked

"Dad, he needs a doctor." Lindy said, but when she turned to the tub, there was only a rumpled pile of towels. At the window, white curtains fluttered.

The screen was pushed out and lay on the lawn below the window. Ada, Lindy and Carson Connors searched the lawn for Stuart. Under the full moon, there were shadows everywhere, but no sign of the boy. The night had gone dead silent. The crickets were now still.

"They say when the crickets stop singing,

winter's coming," he said, in a way that told Lindy his thoughts were on something other than the weather.

"Winter? It's September," Aunt Ada said, "Where's the boy?"

"Put on a pot of coffee," her dad said. "I'll help the Sergeant look for Stuart. We'll be back soon for a piece of that apple pie."

They never got back that night for pie.

The police combed the neighborhood first, then the old Schroeder farm. The State Police were called. They brought dogs and broadened the search.

Posters appeared on telephone poles: Have you seen this boy?

"Hey, Babe." Robbie Stoddard undid his top button and loosened his tie, as he crossed the patio with the cocktail pitcher. Ice chimed against the glass. He kissed Lindy atop the head, nodded to his father-in-law and joined them under the brazen moon.

"My hero," she said, as he topped off her martini.

"That's me." Robbie sat down, stretched his legs long, crossed them at the ankles, and poured himself a drink.

Over the rim of her glass, Lindy stared at the

defect in the hedge.

Over the years, Lindy's thoughts frequently turned to Stuart. That night, Robbie had explained to Lindy and Aunt Ada, what he'd told Carson and the police. That the story Stuart shared about the root cellar at Schroeder's farm was true- but for one important fact. It was *Stuart*, not Robbie, who had been dragged below by the evil thing they disturbed. Stuart had come back changed, hunting for Robbie. Robbie eluded him by ducking into a tool shed beyond Lindy's hedges. That's when Stuart stumbled upon her in the back yard. "You see," Robbie had told them, "he got you to invite him into your house to draw me out. He knew I'd come save you."

"Save us from what," Lindy asked, with a shudder.

"I don't know. From whatever we set loose in that root cellar."

The abandoned farm belonged to the town, since old man Schroeder, who lived his last few decades as a hermit, died. He was the last of his kin and owed all kinds of taxes. Until Robbie and Stuart uncovered the root cellar, no one- at least no one who was still alive- knew about it.

When the police went to the root cellar that night looking for Stuart, they found an oblong hole, long enough and deep enough to hold a casket. In the most recessed corner of the room, they found a dirty white tennis shoe. It matched the sneakers Stuart was wearing the night he disappeared.

So the police replaced the lock and boarded the root cellar to keep others away. Robbie had insisted they replace the silver crucifix first. Sergeant Williams had assured Lindy and her dad, that it was merely to pacify the boy, but something told her that the cops thought it was a good idea, too. Robbie scoured the brush along the edge of the woods with a young deputy, until he found where the cross had landed. The honor of replacing it was left up to the officer. Ill at ease, the deputy crossed himself - Father, Son and Holy Ghost- took a step or two down, and tossed the crucifix into place.

There's a spare room on the third floor in the Connor-Stoddard house. A galaxy of clippings and clues collected over two decades orbits the photograph of a smiling sixteen-year-old boy pinned to the wall. In this room, Lindy revisits the investigation and pours over the details of Stuart's disappearance. On occasion, her dad and Robbie join her. They'll share a pot of coffee, maybe a piece of pie, and deconstruct that strange day.

Tonight, warmed by a cold swallow of gin, she watched Robbie and her dad banter. They'd be happier if she'd put away the faded Polaroid of Stuart, his features now hard to distinguish. Taking down his picture would lessen the nightmares about padlocks and dirt chambers and buried things. Maybe she'd finally call the landscaper to fix the hedge, but she'd never forget. Stuart was somewhere, alive or dead, or somewhere in between. She'd never stop wondering what other evil things wait below the cities and towns in which we live. What else lies in dark, quiet places for the unwary to set them free?

The Bracelet

By

SJ Garman

I drew in a deep breath, allowing the cold morning air to clear my head. Trudging over the mounds of snow which had accumulated in the hospital parking lot overnight, I opened the car door and set down my secret weapon to get home after another double shift: a cup of Karen's horrible coffee syrup. It was the boiled down dregs left over in the nurses' lounge. It was bad, but the jolt of caffeine kept me wide awake.

I hadn't even backed out of my space before the snow started to fall. Dawn was still an hour away and the sliver of moon was quickly vanishing behind a bank of dark clouds. Having driven this route twice daily, I often joked that my car could drive itself through the back country roads towards home. As I sipped Karen's swill, my eye caught movement along the right side of the road. As I drove closer, I saw an old woman struggle to walk over the piles of snow, her legs and arms flailed in an unsuccessful attempt to keep her balance.

I slammed on my brakes, sending the car careening into the ditch, spilling the dark and bitter brew over my uniform and driver's seat. The airbags deployed, leaving my chest and side bruised. Grabbing my purse, I forced my car door open and bounded over the snowbank to the limp figure of the woman lying on the shoulder of the road in front of my vehicle. She looked ancient; her leathery brown face was covered with wrinkles as the snow gently landed on her sparkling white hair.

"Are you alright?" I asked, pushing her bracelet aside to take her pulse. "My name is Sharon and I'm a nurse. I'm here to help you."

"No," she moaned, pulling her arm away, "Don't touch…"

It was too late. The bracelet glowed a blinding blue, making my eyes water. There was something crawling up my hand. The bracelet had transformed into a spider, and its legs clamped around my wrist. I yelled in pain as the thin, black spider bit me, causing blood to stream down my hand and fingers, dripping onto the snow. I attempted to pry the creature's legs off of my arm, but they were imbedded into my flesh. The spider had been alive seconds before, but now was cold to the touch, its red eyes sightless.

"Get it off me!" I yelled, hitting the now shiny, ebony bracelet on the icy road, trying to break it apart.

"I can't," she said weakly. "It must have sensed I'm dying. I'm so sorry."

"Sorry for what?" I snapped. "Just take it back. I'll call for help and you'll be fine."

I fished through my purse for my phone. No cell service. I pulled at the legs of the bracelet, but they were as strong as steel. Then I grabbed a pen out of my pocket to pry the thing off of my wrist.

"It won't work," the woman said. She held out her right arm, showing multiple scars where the bracelet had been. "It selected you. It won't release unless the host is close to death."

"Host?" I asked, "Why me?"

"You touched it," she replied, "It accepted you." She glanced at her bare right forearm and whispered, "It will give you the power to heal."

"I can heal you?" I asked, picking up her hand.

Instantly, the black bracelet changed color, glowing brilliantly, as every joint in my body ached.

"No!" yelled the woman, slapping my hand away.

Streaks of brown now appeared in her white hair and her cheeks were fuller. Glancing down, the veins in my hands were visible now and my skin was speckled with light brown spots.

"What happened?" I asked, touching my hand in disbelief.

"To give a life force to someone, it takes from you. It drains the life out of its host and transfers it to others, keeping them healthy and young." The woman stood up and brushed herself off, looking stronger than she was moments before. "Do you see the stand of pines to the west? Next to it is a cottage that was my grandmother's home. I don't think they know it exists. Here are the keys for the front door. Take her car and anything you can use in the house. Grandma used to keep money in an old cookie jar. Grab it and drive as far away as you can. Don't go home. Turn off your cellphone and ditch it so they can't track you."

"Who are you talking about?" I asked, "How will they find me? Could they help get this thing off of me?"

"How old do you think I am?" she asked.

"Before the bracelet glowed, I would've guessed mid-eighties. Now, you look around sixty."

She sighed, pulling a key ring out of her coat pocket. "Look at the picture," she said, handing me the key ring, "That picture was taken at my high school graduation six months ago. I'm nineteen."

I stared at the picture of the smiling, brown haired girl who was three years younger than me. She had a port wine stain on her forehead, the purple fingers extending beyond her hairline. I looked up to see that the old woman's hair covered most of the purple discoloration, but the birthmark was visible beyond the white strands.

"They grabbed me when I was out jogging one morning. I'm not exactly sure who they were, but I did see some people in military uniforms there. They blindfolded me and forced me to heal people until I became too old and weak. I heard them talking about needing to find someone else to wear it. They thought it wasn't necessary to have more than one guard watching me anymore because I was so old," she smiled broadly. "They were wrong."

"How did you get here?"

"I stole a car," she replied. "I might look like I'm ninety, but I still remember how to hotwire a car. I'd planned to escape to my grandmother's abandoned cottage and drive her old beat-up car until I found someone who could help me to undo all of this." She gestured to her body.

"I can't just leave everything behind," I said. "What about my parents and family? My friends?"

"They'll find your damaged car and won't stop until they've got that bracelet."

"Then I'll give it to them," I replied.

"The bracelet selected you, so you can't give it

back." She took a ragged breath. "They'll threaten your family. You'll be locked away and will never see the light of day again, just as they did with me. They'll drain your life away until you're dead."

The woman slowly wiped the melting snowflakes from her cheek. I heard sirens in the distance.

"They're coming," she said, touching my name badge. "I'd wanted to be a nurse, too. I didn't think this would happen..." She cleared her throat, brushing off the snow from her jacket. "I'll lead them away so you can get to the cottage. Take the car and drive as fast as you can. The snow and wind are picking up, which should help to cover our tracks."

I could hear the sirens getting closer.

"Run."

I turned back to see her disappear into the woods, running the opposite direction from me. As I jogged toward the tall pine tree, I debated about going back. Maybe this was some type of elaborate hoax; a really bad joke. The snow was falling steady now, making the group of trees more difficult to locate. The wind bit through me as the flakes swirled around my face, chunks of ice fell into my tennis shoes and melted, making my feet numb. The storm was building, causing the snow to swirl around me. Just as I was about to turn around, I saw a clearing two hundred yards ahead.

The small house reminded me of the fishing cottages that dotted the shorelines on the lakes where I grew up. Its paint was peeling, the screens were filled with spider webs, and the porch was sagging. The windows were dark and the snow was pushed up against the front door by the wind. No tracks going in or out. There was a small detached garage about three hundred feet away.

I walked up to the door, pushed the snow away with my foot, and slipped the key into the lock. The hinges squeaked in protest as I forced it open. The antique light switch on the wall gave a distinct click when I pushed it in, but nothing came on. The room smelled musty and dank, covered with dust. The sunlight through the dirty windows barely provided enough light to see by. The cupboards were bare, except for cans of soup and green beans, and a box of tea bags that I placed on the countertop. The cookie jar was in the corner: a brown rabbit dressed in a cowboy outfit. Carefully lifting its head, I peered inside. Rolls of ones, fives, and tens were wedged inside for safekeeping. I pried out the money and counted it: $347. The table in the corner of the kitchen had a small bouquet of dead wildflowers on it, the petals and leaves littering the surface around the vase. The wood stove stood silent in the corner, the wind howling down the stovepipe. The only other room was a bedroom with a single bed, carefully covered with a handmade patchwork quilt. A battery operated radio sat on the bedside table with a picture of a smiling little girl who was waving for the camera. A little girl with a port wine stain on her forehead.

I picked up a handmade birthday card next to the bedside table with a picture of a cake on the front. Inside, a child's uneven printing read, "Hapy burthday gramma. Love, Sara." Setting the card down next to the picture, I tried my phone again, but there were no bars. Reaching forward, I turned on the radio, allowing the static to fill the room.

Maybe I should go back to the road. What if the old woman was freezing to death? I should've followed her and not let my imagination get the better of me. What was I thinking?

I adjusted the setting to a local station, hoping to hear something about the storm. Instead, the music was interrupted by a special report. "The police are asking everyone be on the lookout for a woman named Sharon Baker, 22, of Cedar Falls. She is being sought for questioning in the murder of an 87 year old woman. She is considered armed and dangerous. Do not approach her. Call authorities immediately if you see her. A picture of her can be found on our website…"

I stood there, too stunned to move. Did they kill her?

I couldn't go home. I couldn't follow the trail back to my car because it was in the ditch. My trail… If they'd found my car, they might be able to follow my footsteps to the cottage. The wind was howling and it was snowing hard, but maybe not enough to hide my trail. I grabbed everything I could and thrust it into two plastic bags: clothing, boots, an old knitted scarf, and the quilt from the bed. My arm swept the canned goods off of the counter top and into the bags, and shoved the rolls of money into my purse.

Closing the door behind me, I trudged through the snow toward the garage. I set down the plastic bags and grabbed the cover off of a metal trash can that stood next to the garage. Digging through the snow, I cleared it away from the garage door, heaved it open, and went inside. An old, blue sedan was backed in, the ashtray heaped with stale, lipstick covered butts. I threw the bags in the back seat, along with my purse. Plunging into the driver's seat, I reached for the ignition, realizing I didn't have the car keys. My hands flew over the visor, the passenger seat, and the floor. Then I reached for the glove box. As it fell open, I saw my salvation tucked inside.

The car chugged, threatening to quit. Careful not to flood the engine, I pumped the gas pedal, coaxing the sputtering engine to life. Black smoke filled the garage as the wind blew it back inside. The gauge showed I had a half tank of gas. I turned off the power to my phone before putting the car into drive, praying the path before me was the driveway. As I pulled onto the road, I glanced down at the shiny, black spider bracelet wrapped tightly around my wrist. For the first time in my life, I was truly alone, venturing toward an unknown future without a cup of Karen's coffee for the road.

Dark and Bitter

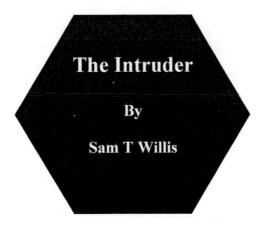

The Intruder

By

Sam T Willis

As I walked away from the funeral, I realized what I wanted. My head was burning with *words*, all the *sounds*, and I was finished with them. I'd never wanted anything more than silence. Everywhere it should have been, I found empty apologies, stifled sobs, and awkward condolences of people who knew—they just *knew*—that they had to say *something*. Only they had no idea *what*. Their faces kept talking long after their voices stopped, and the words weighed as much as an overturned car. I needed to find where the silence was hiding.

So I went to my *place*.

A few months before the accident—when everything was easier—I managed to get six hundred acres of old-growth forest, a good-sized stream, and a beautiful pond, all for dirt cheap at auction. Everyone told me it was a hell of a deal. I was bidding against a guy who'd taken a shot at every lot that day—he always lost interest after two or three times around—and everyone else was wary. I couldn't believe my luck. My very own paradise, and the perfect place to disappear. No one would even be able to find it. The access road was practically invisible.

If I went up there ready to disappear into the woods and simply cease to be, maybe everyone would forget the *something* they needed to say. Maybe I'd forget there was a reason to say anything at all. Way back into the woods, long after I'd run out of dirt road, there was an old, sprawling house—a mansion, really—a large portion of which had fallen in on itself. The addition, one that looked like someone had added it a century after the house was built, was the only part that had remained relatively intact, though it, too, was on the way down. The whole thing was roped off; layer upon layer of yellow tape crying "CAUTION" and "ASBESTOS" lay on the ground. Perhaps someone thought that if they just used enough tape, the house would cease to be. I picked up a length of warning and stuffed it in my pocket. I wasn't afraid of the mansion the way everyone else at the auction was. If the ruin kept them away it would keep the rest of the world away. It was my salvation.

I didn't bring any food—I couldn't remember the last time I'd had an appetite—just a bottle of wine, a bag of coffee, and enough supplies to brew it over a fire. I hiked further into the woods, away from the house, until I found a circle of rocks near the bank of the stream. I'd wanted to camp there since I first found it, but I'd never had the chance. I took the wine bottle out, smashed the neck off on a rock, and dumped it into the stream, watching the wispy trails of red float away. Goodbye. No more wine, not ever. Not that it took any of the blame off. Grasping the body just beneath the shoulder, I held what remained beneath the surface of the stream then watched the clear, cold water pulse out. Wine into water. Neat trick.

I released the remains and turned back to my little camp. It was the perfect spot. Except there were too many birds. They wouldn't shut up, and I was just so damn tired. I built a fire, smashed some coffee beans between two rocks, filled the percolator in the stream, added the grounds, and put it on to boil. After a few impatient minutes I was chewing on the remaining beans themselves. The dark and bitter crunch was the only thing that could drown out the chirping. When the sun went down—maybe—I could sleep.

The crying woke me. The crying and horrible laughing. My eyes opened to the stars, and my ears filled with wild yapping. *Talking.* They were right on top of me and excited, signaling to each other as they ripped up my backpack in search of food they'd never find. In search of sustenance. I lay there in silence and watched, too tired to be afraid. There were dark, shining droplets soaking into the ground near my head—saliva, or blood, that had dripped from their mouths, or coffee I'd spilled when I fell asleep. They didn't seem to even know I was there. They just kept tearing at the canvas, spilling my meager supplies across the ground. I watched the coals, behind them, bleeding their last bits of light into the woods and waited for them to leave me alone.

The fire was dead and the sky was dark before they gave up, and, spurred on by the unnatural levels of caffeine now coursing through them, took off into the woods. I had no idea how late it was and no interest in finding out. Sleep was gone, the coyotes were still howling in the distance, and it was as good as morning for me. I kicked up off the flattened grass and started walking.

There was no conscious decision involved, no thought process I was aware of, but my feet carried me through the woods to the clearing where the old mansion waited. The sight of the thing, naked and jagged, beams sticking up and silhouetted against the moonlight, made my stomach twist. It must have been beautiful, until neglect choked the life from it. There was nothing inside me but coffee and acid.

One of the doors, the one nearest me, had been split in half by the weight of the sagging roof and squeezed open like the door of a crushed car. The inside, an open space that resembled a garage, or a carriage house, was darker than the woods. There wasn't any light seeping in from behind me, just two shafts of moonlight coming in through the back windows that allowed me to see the monstrous pile of garbage that filled the room. Boxes, broken appliances, black garbage bags that shuddered in the wind, overturned couches and chairs: they covered the entire floor at least three feet deep—double that in a few places. Everything that was close enough to see clearly was lined with scratches—the coyotes had already worked the place over—and smelled of mold and rot. To the left of me the walls groaned.

The door that led from this room into the main house was completely blocked by the pile. I climbed up, choosing my footing carefully, and worked my way over to the wall. It would take too long to pull enough of the bags out of the way to get the thing open. Longer than the house had left, I assumed. Just over my head, seven feet above the debris, a storage loft ran the width of the space. I grabbed hold of the edge of it and pulled myself part of the way up, to test the strength of it and see what was up there. More garbage: old toys—mostly dolls— broken and soiled and looming in the darkness. They were staring back at me. A hundred sets of eyes, frozen and pointed at the intruder. I climbed the rest of the way up to spite them.

The pile-up in the loft was less daunting than the one below; I could see the floor in places. There was a door leading into the rest of the house there, directly above the one that was blocked off, and all I had to do was kick a chalkboard and two broken dollhouses over the edge to open it. Wasn't even locked.

The hallway on the other side was windowless and black. I had to run my left hand along the wall and drag my feet to go any further. The carpeting squished with every step, releasing decay into the air. I pulled my shirt over my face and started opening every door I came across. The hall was slanted downwards, steeply, as if inviting me to venture in further, to ignore the rooms on my left and right. Up ahead the structure moaned in protest. I was hurting it. It was more exhausted than I was. The smell was overwhelming; it wasn't long before I had to empty my stomach. I could see only a few feet ahead; there was no way to tell how far the hallway went.

The ceiling sloped down more dramatically than the floor, the walls were bent over, and studs were snapped in places. It seemed every other step I'd catch on something: a nail in the ceiling grazed my head, splinters sticking out of the walls tore my jacket, and my foot got caught in a spot where the floorboard had fallen away. The house coughed, everything shifted an inch—it felt like falling—I steadied myself, freed my foot, and found the door at the end of the hall. I had to use my shoulder to force it open—the jamb was compressed by the partially-collapsed ceiling. Beyond the door the roof was gone. I was essentially outside again, standing at the top of a staircase and listening to the wind in the trees.

I sat down on the top step and considered the rest of the flight. After meandering crookedly downward, the stairwell stopped short of the ground floor, broken near the bottom by an uprooted oak. It had fallen over the back wall and rolled until it was nearly upside-down, its massive tangle of roots reaching up toward me in the quiet desperation of a creature too dumb to know it was over. It was only getting colder, and the weight of the accident, the funeral, the *noise*, was starting to pull me down. I was just so *tired*. I closed my eyes for a second.

When I opened them I couldn't see. My face

was pressed into something hard by something harder, and the darkness was complete. One of my arms was pinned to the stairs below me, but the other was free. I groped around until I understood. My head was pinned between the tree and the stairs—I must have fallen. It had rained while I was sleeping, my head and neck felt wet, and I could smell the copper of the pipes in the ruined walls. But there was no pain. After the accident there was no pain. Except for mine.

It took a long time, but I found the angle and pulled my head free. The stairwell seemed very tall from below; it vanished into a black and soggy expanse. My mouth was still lined with bitterness and grit, and I found my right arm wasn't listening to me. A casualty of the fall. The only way past the tree trunk was to climb over—and it kept *moving*—but the stairs were too tall to consider. The first floor was safer; there was nowhere else to fall.

Beyond the tree—through a hole in the roof-turned-floor—there was a glow. I climbed down through the gap and found walls that were still standing. I was inside again, and I followed the light through a room that was too damaged to identify, and then into a butler's pantry. It was three times as wide as a man, filled in every imaginable space with cabinets, each one open to display the china and mouse skeletons. The ceiling had mostly fallen free of the rafters. There was a lit candle sitting on the counter, next to a sink that had been buried under plaster and laths. I stared at it for a long time, because it couldn't be there. No one would climb through that house. It was *my* house. I picked it up—half in a rage—and it slipped through my slick fingers and fell to the ground, snuffing itself. The darkness was restored and everything felt more *right*. Everything but the intruder. The house agreed with me, grunting its approval, for we had an understanding. I was there to protect it, to usher it quietly to its end, and this person was an enemy of that quiet.

After blindly running my hand through the drawers under the counter, I found something heavy and sharp, traced the blade back to the handle, and gripped it tightly, not allowing my wet fingers to fail. There was only one way through the butler's pantry: into a narrow corridor that led down a set of stone steps, around a corner, and down further into the cellar kitchen. There was more candlelight there, illuminating a room that—being mostly underground—was better preserved than the rest of the house. The floor was dirt or stone and the walls were the same, and at the back of the room, something moved. The enemy. If it—if he or she or *it*—wanted light, then I wanted dark. I didn't need to see any more. I just needed to keep moving. One-by-one, my knife knocked the candles from their sticks, I ground the wicks out with my feet, and the wax coating the bottom of my shoe grew thicker and thicker. It felt like stepping on flesh. The enemy wasn't moving fast; it wanted me to follow. It didn't know the house was on my side.

I took off my jacket and left it on the floor. It seemed to be restricting my movements. Stifling me. I was better off without it. Colder, but better. Through the back of the kitchen more stairs, lower ceilings, more candles. Everything glowed. The hall under the kitchen was a tunnel of smooth, carefully-hewn stones that wound round and down, like a snake burrowed into the earth. The enemy was always just ahead; I caught a flicker of movement around every corner, and I resolved to walk faster. The floor was slick with running water. Every step was more effort than the last. My feet were heavier, the water was deeper, and the air was thicker and reeked of decay and rotting wine. I passed racks and racks of it, all along the hall, bottles freshly broken at the neck and dripping red vinegar into the river. This couldn't be under the house any longer—it felt like I'd walked for miles—and I just wanted to sit down.

Before long, I realized it was more cave than tunnel. I'd left the racks behind, and water was running down the walls, through shining troughs in ancient limestone deposits and down to the shin-deep, freezing water. I hadn't seen a candle for a thousand feet or more, but still the cave was illuminated by an unseen light just a little further down the path. It kept winding around and down, on and on. Here was real, palpable, intoxicating silence. The water ran slowly and was barely louder than my breath. Even the stench was dissolving as I walked; the rot, wine, and pipes couldn't follow me. If only I could snuff the light, this would be the place to disappear. The house and I could rest, just as soon as I caught the intruder.

The water was past my knees when the stone hall opened into a large, round chamber, and the floor dropped sharply from there. Straight ahead of me was a person's back: a long, dark coat hanging down and refusing to float in chest-deep water like its pockets were full of stones. Below the surface, all around him or her or *it*, were tiny glowing figures on the walls. I couldn't tell if they were carved in or painted, but there were hundreds of them. Impossibly ornate, tiny people with wide eyes and open mouths that moved ever-so-slightly with each ripple of the freezing water's surface. Like they were just waiting to say *something*. The more I stared, the more of them I could see. I leaned in closer to see what they were made of.

Water flooded into my eyes. It was in my nose and ears. Did I fall asleep? Wispy trails of wine were sinking below me, dancing their way toward the bottom. I was looking straight down—dead-man's float—at the hundreds or thousands of glowing figures that stared up from the floor. My muscles were so stiff from the cold, it felt as though I couldn't move at all, and the knife had fallen from my hand. It was lying four feet below my face in the grip of those creatures of light. I let as much time pass as I could. The air in my lungs went stale. I put my feet back on the ground and my head pulled itself out of the water, leaving the knife on the ground for the figures. The intruder was gone. Beyond the place it had stood, the passage went on through a low and wide opening. It rose only a foot or so above the surface of the water. In the dim light of the glowing figures, I began to see a relief cut into the stone wall surrounding it. It was carved to look like a vast mouth—gaping wide and smiling—drawing the underground river and all the glowing people into itself.

Consuming them.

The enemy had gone that way. I was sure of it. My body was numb and shaking with cold and exhaustion. The water stung my eyes. Peace was just a little further down the corridor. I just had to catch the intruder. The tiny faces in the water, I could see then, were staring at the gigantic mouth with a kind of fixed terror as the flowing water pulled them in.

The floor disappeared in blackness when I reached the mouth, and I had to swim to keep my head above the surface. With one arm and no strength left, I followed the low, dark corridor. The glow faded to nothing. The walls pressed in, leaving less and less room for my head. The numbness took over. There was no rotting smell. There was no pain.

There was no wine and there was no walking away. I pressed on through the water in perfect, *silent* darkness. All the faces and all the words faded. I was sure it was just a little further. I closed my eyes.

Dark and Bitter

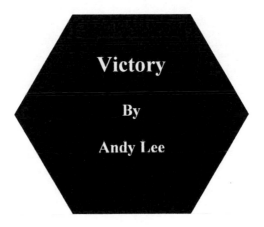

Maybe the rage was in him all along, held back by fragile threads. It's possible his tumultuous teen years caused critical failure, a synaptic cascade that began with impulsivity at twelve, and ended with newspaper headlines at seventeen. In his own mind, Victor did not perceive the collapse.

Those who attempted to explain found no rationale. He was not especially bullied, unlucky, unloved, or even, until then, unliked. Up to that point, he'd been interested in robotics, video games, baseball, and held down a job at Paco's Tacos for one year and eight months. He had his driving permit, had taken the PSAT's, and done well enough that his parents did not think he'd need tutoring to get into college. They all expected that he'd get into college. But when he broke, Victor shattered entirely and he left his spatter pattern on many lives.

It was bitingly blue at the bus stop; the sun not yet up, the moon already down. Periodic gusts brought frost to Victor's lips. His eyes crackled, his nose dripped. He stomped, and felt the weight of the knife in his jacket. It felt strong, unbending against his ribs. In the morning when he was dressing, he'd seen it on his dresser, still sharp even after shaving the bark off the branch he'd picked to whittle. Something numb and unthinking told him to bring it that day. There, in the aphotic dawn of his typical life, Victor let go of his hold on decency, morality, reality.

When the school bus arrived, all the driver found was Corey Landsdowne lying in dark bloody snow. The driver stared for half a minute. The cold air blew in through the open bus door, up the steps and down the shocked aisle. It was the first time the kids had ever seen their driver stand up and hustle down the steps.

Cory lay on his side, so she immediately saw the knife sticking out of his blue winter jacket. The blood wasn't coming from there, though. When she rolled him over, she saw the gash across his face and neck, deep enough to show tissue and bone.

The driver recoiled, hastily climbing back up the steps. She called on the radio for assistance, then grabbed her jacket and pulled her cell phone from the pocket. Jumping back down, the driver dialed 911, cradling the phone as she spread her jacket over the boy, tucking it in around him. He was still alive, gurgling bloody bubbles. His eyes were glazing over and dilated.

Kneeling down in the snow, the mother of three pulled as much of the boy as she could onto her generous lap, shielding him from the wind and snow. Boys came to the top of the steps, looking down at her. The look in her eyes, the timber of her screech, sent them scurrying.

Corey gurgled and stared at the lightening sky, laying in the driver's lap, but was DOA by the time the ambulance loaded him up. The District sent out a car with an extra driver, who took over the bus route. The first driver, covered now in blood and soaking wet, climbed, shaking, into the vehicle, and was taken home.

After finishing off Corey, Victor jogged home and retrieved his dead grandfather's shotgun from the garage. Boxes of bullets sluiced down from the high wooden shelf when he stood on his toes to reach them. He filled all of his pockets, and then filled up the gun, side by side double barrel. The boxlock break action was well oiled. He wished he had something better, faster than the twelve gauge, but it would do. He felt a flush on his skin, his neck hot in the winter cold. He flipped the safety off and walked out of the open garage.

Three houses down was old Mrs. Willis. He didn't bother to ring the bell. When the front door knob wouldn't turn, he used one shot to blast through the handle, then pushed the door open with the toe of his boot and marched into the house. He had more confidence than he'd ever felt, the gun smooth in his hands.

He found her upstairs, alert to his strange

noises but sitting still in her armchair. She looked so typical, dressed in her pale blue bathrobe and thin slippers, her steely hair still wrapped in some kind of hair net. Her mouth was a grim line and her eyes flashed angry, but the old woman said nothing. On her lap was a cat that she grasped a little too tightly. When he pushed through the doorway, it leaped off her and scurried behind a filing cabinet. Beside her on a small table a mug sat steaming.

Victor watched as the cat fled, then cocked the cast-off wooden stock snug to his shoulder and fired directly into her shocked, wrinkled face. As he wiped the blood from his parka with a bathroom towel, he realized he'd have to stand a little further back from his next target. He tossed it to the kitchen floor on his way to the back door.

He climbed over the low stone fence to the house directly behind Mrs. Willis. A large mix-breed dog came running toward Victor, barking. Stupid dog was always barking. He lifted the gun and popped off the dog in motion. Victor's hat flew off with the recoil, his black hair, sweaty and long, danced in motion before he recovered. He smiled at his success, that dog could have easily jumped him. He left the hat in the wet snow.

The kitchen door was ajar, the glass door shut. He opened it as if he was walking into his own home and saw a mousy haired woman sitting with a little boy in a high chair, pulled up to the kitchen table. He cocked, fired, and felt again the blush of passion, feeling the kick of the gun against his body, smelling the hot powder and the steel and the oil. He watched the spray of her blood against the wall behind her, pop art on the pale paint. She shook and landed prostrate on the floor, the boy's chair sliding a few feet away as she knocked into it, but it did not fall over He walked out the front door and crossed the street, hearing the boy bleat behind him. He strode, focusing on the sound of his boots on the paving stones, and added shells from his pocket to the shotgun. He was completely in control, feeling an addictive rush of energy.

In the next house lived an old couple. She was on the phone in the kitchen when the shotgun blasted through her, spreading her smile across the Formica table. Teeth popped and smacked into the window beside the sink. Victor hung up the phone for her. He surprised her husband upstairs in the bathroom, where he sat, half asleep and probably deaf.

The fourth house had three children and a harried mother. The mother had already locked the doors. The children whined and wailed. He put them all out of their misery, using only four bullets. They made a stinking mess, his boot soles challenged by the glistening slick. He was careful as he left, wiping his feet thoroughly on their hall carpet.

He reloaded before each house, until he had no more shells. He knew he could go back to his own house for more ammo, but he was spent. He felt the flush turn clammy and the cold penetrate his bones. The weight of consequence strangled him, made him gasp for frozen air, paralyzing his lungs.

The police found him sitting on back porch steps, a quarter of a mile of carnage from his own house. They had spread out across the neighborhood, keeping people inside, trying to keep everyone safe. No one tried to be a hero, the incomprehensibility was too thick.

Victor could see the officers poking their faces through the bushes to his right, could hear them in the house behind his back. He could still taste the heat of the metal muzzle and the heavy, burning smell of flesh; the memory of that sustained him for those last few moments. He rested the gun stock on the bottom step and leaned into the end of the barrel, gagging as it slid down past his epiglottis so that he could reach the primed trigger. He didn't need to force himself, he could do this, in spite of the discomfort.

He heard the heavy pounding as they came closer to the door behind him, and Victor knew there were men in the bushes pushing through the foliage. His ass was so cold, sitting on the frozen wood. He squeezed the trigger.

The round blew his neck out against the wall of the porch, spattering viscera onto the pant legs of the officer barging through the rear door. The shotgun landed with a clunk. Everyone stood still.

In the earliest light of that cold, sour day, Victor was done. Twenty six spent shells, twenty four people killed from seven families. Between them all, more than eight hundred forty-three people attended the wakes and funeral services.

But for Victor, only his parents stood, perplexed and beside the deep frozen grave of their son. Cold rain and snow melted against their faces.

Victory

Stock still, they watched as he was lowered into the dark and bitter soil.

Dark and Bitter

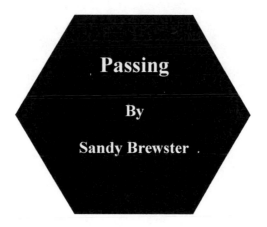

Passing

By

Sandy Brewster

At six a.m. Sunday morning, Miranda rang her great-grandmother's doorbell. Ann swung the door open and beamed at her.

"Well, here you are, bright and early, and Gigi's wide awake! She'll be so pleased to see you." When Miranda was small, "great-grandma" had been hard to say, so she'd been encouraged to call her "Gigi". Gigi had begun to call the little girl "Miri", and it'd been "Gigi and Miri" ever since.

"Hello," Miranda said, walking past the woman into the house.

It didn't faze Ann. "Nancy, look who's here!" she said, following Miranda into the living room. "I'm going to go have a cup of coffee and leave you girls to talk."

Miranda rolled her eyes and focused on her great-grandmother. The head of the hospital bed was slanted up and Gigi was smiling. She looked even smaller than she had the day before.

"Miri," she whispered, her voice was dry and rattly.

"Hi, Gigi," Miranda replied, not hearing her own words. She moved closer to the bed, cleared her throat and tried again. "Hi, Gigi, I hoped we could talk about the old journal you gave me."

Gigi smiled again, but her lips fell back into a slack droop before Miranda could walk the final step to Gigi's side. She sat in the chair next to the bed and gently stroked the thin, blue veined hand that lay inside the rail.

"I've been reading about your train ride to school, and Penelope and her brothers, and all the stuff you did."

Gigi nodded.

"Did Penelope ever come to visit you? Did you make the debate team?" Miranda waited for Gigi to answer a question or make a comment.

Although the bright blue eyes were still locked on the girl's, Gigi didn't say a word. Her lips moved and Miri leaned closer, watching carefully. The thin light brown lips met and separated, moving out at the ends.

"Read," Miri repeated, nodding, and pulled the old notebook out of her bag. She opened it where Penelope's drawing marked her place and began reading:

"When they build a new building, people put things in an empty stone in a corner of the foundation. Penelope told me about it, it's called a time capsule. Usually they will put in a newspaper, coins with the date on them, and items that represent their culture at the time. That's what she thinks we should do, make a time capsule. We wouldn't put it in a

building of course, but we could put it
in a metal box and bury it. Maybe our
grandchildren will find it."

Miri looked up. "Gigi, did you do it? Did you
guys bury a time capsule?"

The old woman's eyes brightened a bit and
she nodded. "Did anyone ever find it?"

The skeletal face turned left then right a
fraction. "No? Do you think it's still hidden where
you put it?"

Gigi smiled and lowered her chin. Her eyes
were drooping, and the light in them was fading in
them. Miri bit her lip, and turned back to the book:

"We're going to talk to the boys and
girls at school tomorrow. We know
we'll put one or two of Mr.
Tillapaugh's newspapers in the box.
And I think Daddy will help us with
the box, he's good at building things. I
don't know what else we'll put in, but
I expect the others will have ideas."

When Miri looked up, Gigi was sound asleep.
Ann was straightening up her chair side table, where
her yarn and needles rested with a notebook, pens,

and a novel. Miri looked at her, and Ann smiled a watery smile.

What's up with that? As soon as Miranda had the thought, she knew she didn't want to know. "There are cookies in the kitchen," Ann told her. "Help yourself."

Miranda went, using the excuse to leave the room. She grabbed her favorite cup from the cupboard, the one with Yosemite Sam with a fading orange mustache. She filled it with water and set it on the table. She reached for the cupboard door where the plates were kept and paused as she heard the doorbell. She recognized her mother's voice as Ann opened the door. Miranda decided she was not ready to go back, and opened the cupboard, taking out a plate with a blue picture on the surface. She traced the basket design on the rim and studied the little people working on the farm pictured in the center. She gave herself a shake and put two cookies on the plate, then sat down at the table, taking a bite.

The voices in the hall flowed on and on, quietly, sometimes louder. Miri could almost understand what was being said, but she didn't want to. She took a drink of water and overheard her mother sadly exclaim, "Oh, Ann!"

Miranda turned on Gigi's huge old CD player. A big band era disc started playing softly. Miri and Gigi used to love to listen to this music, and Gigi had taught her a couple of her favorite dances. Miri turned up the volume and sat back down, drinking the rest of her water. She picked up the cookie with the bite taken out and crumbled it onto the plate, pushing the crumbs around to circle first one tiny person in the plate's design, then another.

"Miranda?" Mom was standing in the doorway.

Miranda stood up quickly and dumped her plate in the trash, putting the dish and glass in the sink. She stood staring at the picture Gigi had hung over the sink, a painting of a window with a farm outside, sheep, horses and cows feeding on rolling green hills. She could hear her mother pull out a chair and settle into it. Miranda straightened the eyelet curtain framing the painting and turned around, sagging back against the counter.

"Miranda," her mother said again.

Why was everybody crying today?

"Dad's coming for you. I'm staying here with

Gigi tonight. The doctor says. . . I don't know if…"
She looked down again, poking at crumbs on the
table.

"I was going to get that!" Miranda snapped,
grabbing a dishcloth. She stomped to the table,
throwing the cloth on its surface.

Her mother put her hand on Miranda's arm.
"Honey…" "I'm okay, Mom. Really. I'm going to be
alright."

Miranda's eyes snapped open. She'd been
dreaming about Penelope's brothers after reading
about the boys in her great-grandmother's journal.

Where was it? She sat up and turned on her
light, scanning her bed and the floor nearby.

Nothing. She twisted and lifted her pillow.
There it was, still open, with one page unnaturally
folded back and creased by the weight of her sleeping
on it. She smoothed the page and lay the book on the
table next to her.

Miranda picked up her phone and unplugged
the charger before settling back against her pillow.

It was three a.m.. *Well, as long as I'm awake*

maybe I should have a snack, she thought.

Padding down the hall barefoot, she saw a light shining from the kitchen. Maybe her Mom was back. Maybe Gigi was resting comfortably, better already. She turned the corner and saw her Dad at the stove and in a rush, she knew she was lying to herself.

Dad was pouring milk into a saucepan. He paused and glanced at her, then poured more milk into the pan.

"Old-fashioned hot cocoa," Miranda said. She remembered Gigi'd always made it for the family on Christmas eve. Gigi also made it on regular days, because it was cold, or because they were celebrating, or because Gigi was sad, or she was just in the mood. Miranda's great-grandmother hadn't been a coffee drinker, she preferred her tea- strong, dark and bitter with nothing added. But on special occasions, she liked this cocoa.

Her Dad turned after placing the pan over low heat on the stove burner. "Do you remember the time she put chili pepper in it after she'd been reading about the Aztecs?" he asked, turning again to pull the baking cocoa out of the cupboard.

"Yes. Mom didn't like it, and Gigi made

another pot for her." Miri opened a drawer and pulled out a slender whisk. "Couldn't sleep?" she asked, trying to keep her voice normal.

He took the whisk. "Your Mom told me on our first date, she made it a practice not to eat foods that could bite her back. I was trying to impress her, so I made reservations at the best restaurant I could find," he hesitated, "a Thai place... I pre-ordered my favorites... total fail."

Miranda usually loved to hear the story over and over, but now she was impatient. She knew Dad had something to tell her, and that he couldn't delay it much longer.

"Mom called," he said

Miranda sank into a chair and clenched her hands. She glared at them, resting on the table, then lowered them to hide them in her lap. *She's gone. She's gone*, she thought over and over, but she wouldn't say it. Maybe that would make it true, and maybe it wasn't true. Yet. She stared at her Dad's face and willed him to say anything except what she was expecting.

He stirred the milk and measured the cocoa and sugar into it, whisking again until it was smooth.

He turned toward Miri. His face was gray and

tired.

He's getting old, Miri thought, then told herself, *stop it*. She didn't want anyone else to get old.

"Miri, honey, Gigi is gone. I didn't want to wake you. A couple of hours wouldn't have changed things."

Miri looked down at her hands, realizing her knuckles were white and wet. Another drop fell on them, and she realized she was crying.

"Baby, she lived a good life, she was tired, she was ready," he said in a rush as he dropped to his knees by her chair, wrapping his arms around her.

She sobbed and gripped his shoulders as tightly as she'd been gripping her fists. For a few minutes nothing could be heard but her crying. The harder she held Dad, the more firmly he hugged her back. Finally she gasped, drawing in air to find her voice. "I know, she told me that. I'm so selfish, I guess I'm crying for myself, not for Gigi."

"Baby, it's okay. Go ahead. I know you're going to miss her. We'll all miss her, but she was special to you. You were very important to her."

"I want to see her."

Dad drew back and studied Miranda's face.

"Don't you want to remember her as she was when she was alive?"

Miranda pulled away and stood up. "I'm sorry, Dad, but that's just stupid. Know what she looked like last time I saw her? Like, like a buzzard! Like a skeleton!"

There was a sizzling sound and a smell of scorching milk. "Oh no! The cocoa!" Miri swung around and grabbed the handle of the pan, throwing it in the sink. Her Dad switched off the heat and stood helplessly gazing at the mess on the stove.

"We can fix it, Dad. Come on, you wipe up the wet stuff on the stove and I'll get what spilled on the floor. Then the burner should be cool enough that we can clean it."

He half-smiled at her, taking the sponge she handed him.

They got the messiest part up, and he started scrubbing the pan as Miranda took apart the burner and cleaned it up. "I don't know what I'll do about this." He held up the pan, showing his daughter the baked-on crud.

Miranda took the pan from him and laughed.

"I know what to do. Gigi taught me how to

clean burnt-on messes." She put baking soda in the pan, added water, set it on a burner and turned the heat up to high. Grabbing another saucepan, she started their old-fashioned hot chocolate again.

She turned back to her father. "Well, will you take me to Gigi?"

He took a deep breath, "Yes. Let me call your Mom and give her a heads up." He went into the living room and Miri stirred the cocoa, adjusting the heat and watching the surface of the warming brown liquid carefully. She reached into the spice rack and lifted down the red pepper, giving the tin a few shakes over the saucepan.

Mom opened Gigi's door, holding a mug of coffee in one hand. She looked like what Gigi would have called "the Wreck of the Hesperus". Miranda wasn't sure what that meant, exactly, although Gigi once recited the old poem for her. She understood it meant a real mess, though, and that's what Mom was. Miranda hugged her tight before Mom pushed her back and intently eyed her daughter.

Taking her daughter's hand, the woman led

her back into the kitchen. "Are you sure about this?" she asked the girl, looking at her carefully again.

Dad had followed her into the room and leaned on the door behind her.

Her mother turned to the stove. "Would you like some old-fashioned hot chocolate first?" She turned the heat up to low under a small pot.

Miranda and her father started laughing. "What?"

"No hot chocolate for us, please." Aaron crossed the room and turned off the burner, pulling his wife into an embrace. "Miranda and I have talked about this, and she knows what she's doing, Lin."

"Is she any worse than yesterday?" Miranda asked.

Mom thought a minute, then replied, "No, actually she looks better."

"Don't tell me she's so 'natural.' They said Madison's grandfather looked 'natural' after he died, and she expected a pile of leaves and sticks when she went to the viewing." Miranda paused. "Are we having a viewing?"

"No, Gigi has donated her body to Albany Medical Center's cadaver program. Students will use it to learn what they are doing before they ever see inside a living person," said Aaron.

"They're coming to pick her up later this morning." Mom rubbed another tear off her cheek. "Oh, I don't want to start this again."

Miranda wondered if Mom had been here alone all night. "Where's Ann?" She asked, feeling her anger rising again.

"After Gigi . . . was gone, I told her to go get some sleep. We had a good cry together, but I didn't need her as much as she needs sleep."

"Can I see her now?" She asked, walking towards the living room.

With one last glance at her husband, Miranda's mother took her hand and led her in by the hospital bed. Gigi looked tinier than she had yesterday, her eyes were closed and she reminded Miri of the way her sweatshirt crumpled when she threw it on the floor in a corner of her room. "She looks peaceful," her mother said.

"No. She's... like a shell now. It's like she told me, she's not there anymore. This is the house she lived in while she was here, and now it's empty. She's not uncomfortable now. It's okay. I think." Miranda sat down in the chair next to the bed and began to cry. "Oh Mom, what am I going to do without Gigi?"

Her mom knelt by the chair and held her. "We're going to miss her like stink. But what would she tell us?"

Miranda laughed through her tears. "She'd say, 'Stop snivelling. Things need doing, now get to it.'"

Her Dad stood in the doorway, laughing. "That's true. And she'd probably remind us to find the joy in the situation. Like maybe in our memories of her."

"Yeah." Miranda wiped her eyes on the tissue Mom handed her. "So what do we need to do first?"

Saturday morning, Miranda woke up exhausted. Her first thought was hoping that the memorial service would represent the "closure" her dad said was the intention. Not that she'd ever forget Gigi, but she was longing for the stage where she'd be able to remember the great times and things she loved about Gigi, without the wrenching pain of having to learn to live without her.

It was raining, which made sense to Miranda. It should rain when there was a funeral for someone as deeply loved as Gigi. Dad had said Gigi had peculiar instructions about the whole thing, but she was kind of shocked with what she saw. In the main auditorium, a slideshow of pictures of Gigi was running on the wall behind the stage. A burst of color was provided by huge bunches of balloons. They were tied on either side of the stage and to the guest book table in the back.

Miranda was still staring open-mouthed when Ann came over and started speaking to her. "What?" Miranda demanded, snapping her mouth closed so she wouldn't resemble a fool.

"I wondered if you'd like to see the fellowship hall before people start arriving." Miranda nodded and followed Ann to the room in the back.

More bunches of balloons were tied everywhere and a large screen was showing the slide show.

The tablecloths were red with purple streamers like road lines stretching the length of the tables. Napkins and silverware were set up in front of each chair, and a tiny bottle was at each place setting as well.

Miranda picked up one of the bottles.

"Bubbles." Ann told her. "She was very clear that we had to have bubbles." Miranda smiled, putting the bottle back on the table.

She remembered going to Gigi's apartment and finding her out on the patio blowing bubbles. Miri had just turned twelve and she wanted to be seen as mature, so she'd sat down and folded her hands in her lap, looking slightly disapproving.

Gigi had glanced at her sideways, blew the wand for one last bubble, then dipped the wand back in the bottle, asking, "Problem?"

"Well, maybe. Aren't we a bit too old to be blowing bubbles?"

"God forbid! I will never be too old for bubbles.- I bet God even has them in heaven."

Miri was soon taking her turn, blowing and popping the bubbles, along with three of Gigi's neighbors.

Ann was talking again. "I have to put my hat on. I think your mom is in the church now, greeting people. Do you want to come with me or go find her?"

Miranda was not ready to greet people. "I guess I'll go with you."

For the first time, she noticed that Ann was wearing purple. Not a subdued, dark purple or even a subtle pastel lilac color, but a dress of bright purple, with a red scarf looped at her neck. Wow. She followed Ann into a small room with coat hooks where Ann opened a round box sitting on a bench. A huge, red feather popped out of the box, revealing a red felt hat with a purple hat band. Miranda gasped.

"Isn't that Gigi's hat?"

Ann laughed softly, lifting it out of the box. "Yes, but she gave it to me, insisting I wear it to her memorial. She knew I'd wear something 'appropriate for a funeral' if she didn't *manage* me." She settled the hat on her head and turned to a dark rectangular mirror. "Well?"

Miranda reached up and smoothed the feather, straightening the hat on Ann's head. "Fine. It looks fine."

Ann squinted at her reflection one more time. "I wouldn't have the nerve if I didn't know she'd made our entire Red Hat chapter swear they would wear their hats."

Music started playing softly in the church. Ann took a deep breath. "Okay, show's on, as she used to say. Let's go." She led the way, opening a door into the front of the church.

The room was full of people, in pews and folding chairs and standing against the walls. Miranda could see glimpses of her mother, hidden now and again by flamboyant red hats. Frantic movement caught Miranda's attention and she looked toward the center aisle where her friends were waving and trying to squeeze their way towards her.

Miranda sat with her friends, right behind her parents.

Mr. Henderson stepped up to the podium and leaned into the microphone. "Welcome, friends and family of Nancy," he boomed, signaling to the sound booth to turn the sound down.

People began settling until every seat was full and a small crowd was still standing. "The ushers say there's room in the fellowship hall and a large screen television will be showing the service live."

A few people in the back slipped out the door as one of the ushers climbed up beside Mr.

Henderson, covering the mic as he talked to the older man.

Gigi's friend, Mr. Henderson turned back,

announcing, "I guess we're nearly full. We'd better get started. But first, a few announcements; As you can see in your program, after a short message, we will open up the floor for your memories. However, Nancy was very adamant that the whole service should take under an hour. Please limit your time to four minutes or less. And if some one by you forgets the rule, you are to pinch them in the elbow until they sit down."

Everyone laughed.

"Don't worry if you don't have a chance to speak, there are three-by-five cards and pens on the tables in the back. If you have a memory you'd like to share, please write it down. Now let's open the service with prayer."

After the prayer, everyone sang "Amazing Grace." Gigi's good friend, Elna, sang "Blessed be the Name."

After the Pastor was done speaking, Mr. Henderson announced he was "opening up the floor" and people began standing up. Mr. Henderson pointed first one direction, then another and each person he pointed to told a story they remembered about Gigi. Most of them kept it short. Sure enough, one hour after Mr. Henderson had first spoke, he put both hands in the air, as if he were shoving people back into their seats.

"Thank you all for coming. There are refreshments in the fellowship hall, thanks to the ladies of the church, the Red Hat club, and the social committee from Euclid Apartments.

Many people decided not to stay when they saw the crowd in the hall, but Miranda's friends lined up with her. "Thanks for coming, guys, and for eating with me," Miranda said, reaching for a plate.

Jacob grinned, piling potato salad on his plate. "Oh, no problem, I'll force myself to eat the free dinner." He paused, eyeing the tables full of people. "Where will we sit?"

"I've got the perfect place." Miranda balanced her full plate in one hand and snagged four bottles of bubbles and headed for the door on the far side of the room. It opened out onto a little porch, and her friends settled along the bench facing the opening.

Miranda stepped out onto the decrepit porch, looking over the valley below. The rain had stopped and the sun was setting, in all the best sunset colors. She pulled out her phone and snapped a few pictures and thought it was an appropriate ending to a day spent remembering someone who was so loved.

Noir

By

Jaz Johnson

With a grunt and a lethargic lift of her head, Vivian Black had once again joined the world of the living.

*Wine should **not** have been invented.*

Thanks, Jesus.

Shifting onto her bare knees, Vivian hissed at the struggle to sit up in her black silk nightgown. One hand clutched at the hardwood, and the other gripped the roots of her curly black hair as she fought to open her eyes. She glared at the floor to find yet *another* wine stain.

Great.

The digital clock above the television in the living room read *Sunday, January 31, 10:43*AM, as the late morning news emanated from the speakers:

"Investigators are still looking for the body of a woman neighbors reported missing last Monday, and presumed dead. There are still currently no leads as to where the woman may have gone, or who may be involved in a possible abduction and murder," the news reporter relayed into her mic as she stood in the midst of the neighborhood in question. *"The victim, a young ..."*

Vivian huffed as she scrubbed at the wine stain on the hallway floor. She swore under her breath after five minutes of no progress. In an effort to better remove stains, she had taken up her carpet – which now seemed to be a wasted effort. Blowing the curls from her forehead, she listened to the news in the background, dunking her brush back in the sudsy water. She glanced up at the screen in time to see the reporter in front of a salmon-pink house surrounded by a white-picket fence and red rose bushes.

"Amateurs," Vivian scoffed, as she dropped the brush in the bucket and sat up, shaking her head. "Search their house!" As a *former* detective herself, she knew the ins and outs of how to handle a missing person's case. And one of the first things to be done with no leads was to search the home of the missing person, following interrogations, of course. Especially if the victim was thought to be dead. "Hell. It's probably the boyfriend. Doubt she's dead. Probably took off like an idiot," she mumbled to herself, rising to her feet. Glaring at the resilient stain, she turned on her heel to walk toward her front door.

"Magic eraser my *ass*," she grumbled to herself as she stepped off her porch. Headed toward the mailbox. She combed her fingers through unruly curls, head still pounding. "I need more wine," she said, as she opened her mailbox in search of the newspaper.

"Sure that's a good idea?" came a voice from across her yard.

Shifting her gaze in its direction, Vivian's hazel eyes met the crisp blue ones of her admirer. Eyes stereotyped with wavy blonde hair and a pearly smile.

"You look like you've had plenty already. Leave the house in that, often?" the stranger asked with a gesturing nod, his eyes daring to travel.

Remembering her current attire, she steadied her weight onto one of her legs, her hand falling from her forehead to perch on her hip as her eyes narrowed. "Only when there's a peeping tom around," she snapped.

Chuckling, he leaned back against her neighbor's picket-fence and gave a nonchalant shrug, challenging her glare with a wink. "Well, I don't know who *Tom* is. But my name's Grant, if you've forgotten," he offered, making Vivian's brows pinch in confusion.

"Forgotten?" Vivian challenged.

"You really *did* have a lot," he sighed. "Maybe you'll remember 'God.' You called it out quite often during …"

"*Oh, shit,*" Vivian groaned, slapping her hand against her face, immediately regretting it when her head pounded in protest.

"Mm, *no*. It was definitely 'God.' Though I remember the nickname 'fuck' here and –"

"*Shut up,*" Vivian sneered. "What are you

doing out here?" *What was he doing in* **me**?

Holding up his hand, he twirled the stem of a thorn-less rose between his index and thumb. "I was *trying* to be romantic."

"You failed."

"Maybe I can make it up inside?"

Vivian paused. "Hurry up." As annoyed and embarrassed as she was at not remembering the one-night stand, the idea of refreshing her memory wasn't a terrible thought. Especially if she had really done all that screaming. The Ken doll must have done something right. Grant gave a smug grin and a waggle of his brows before Vivian rolled her eyes and gestured towards the house.

"Hand it over," Vivian ordered, gesturing to the paper in the stranger's hands as he approached the sofa of the living room. The TV was still playing, the news on a loop. He had picked up the paper and her mail for her on their way inside.

Grant reached for the remote left on the sofa and changed to a sports channel before glancing between her and the pile in his hand. He smirked, scoffing. "What, you don't want to look at your bills first?" he challenged.

"Bills will be there tomorrow. But the news will change."

"You don't seem like the type to be too concerned."

"And you don't seem like the type to fuck worth a damn. But we're both *full* of surprises, aren't we?" she snipped, arms crossing. Her expression fell when seeing his increasingly smug one. She frowned, eyes narrowing. "Utter *any* part of that joke and it'll be the last thing you do."

"Somehow, I doubt that."

"*Give me the paper.*"

"So you can *ignore* me like you did all last night? No way," Grant complained, tossing the paper – and her mail – over the sofa and onto the floor.

Vivian glared. *What was she thinking?* She really *did* need to stop drinking.

"Excuse the hell out of me for passing out. I'm sure that didn't stop you from having your fun," Vivian accused.

"*Fuck you,* very much. I'm not a rapist," Grant spat back, turning off the television. "Unless, of course," he smiled. "You're into that sort of thing."

"Where the fuck did we even *meet?*" Vivian roared, fed up with his smart-alecky remarks. "Just how many bottles ..."

"Three. And you picked me up at a liquor store."

Another pounding face palm. *Classy, Vivian. Real classy.* "Of course I did."

"Quite persuasive, for a drunk –"

Cutting off his next round of insults, Vivian pushed him back against the sofa before dragging his body half onto the floor, leaving his upper torso to lay against the cushion, his head propped against the crease. His lashes fluttered, lips curving into a smile at the sudden change in action as Vivian knelt onto the sofa, her legs spreading to straddle the stranger's face, effectively shutting him up.

"Why don't you do me a favor and try putting that mouth to *good* use?" she scowled, arms resting over the back of the sofa as she pressed her hips down and raked her fingers through her hair again to sooth her pounding temple.

"You really are deserving of your name," Vivian sighed, as she flopped back against the sofa. She had turned around to sit properly, while Grant had knelt in front of her to carry out her request – and a second orgasm. "Maybe my tastes aren't fading after all."

Grant scoffed, wiping his thumb across his lips before standing up with a smug grin. "You seemed to favor 'Fuck' this time around."

"Don't ruin the moment," Vivian groaned, before standing up to stretch. Again, her hand reached up to clutch at her aching head. "Fucking *three* bottles. Why didn't you stop me? I could have *died.*"

Grant shrugged. "You seemed to be able to hold it until you dropped."

That reminded her. "Feel like making yourself useful a third time?" Vivian offered, glancing toward her hallway at the bucket and stain she had left behind. "I'll return the favor if you can get that stain out," she offered, gesturing towards Grant's responding manhood. But to her surprise, he shook his head no as he plopped himself back onto the sofa.

"You spill it, you clean it."

"*Little shit*," she grumbled before trudging off to try her second attempt at removing the stain. "Maybe if I soak it…" she went on, passing the hall to go into the kitchen in search of bleach.

Grant's expression slowly faded as he watched her go, the gleam in his eyes morphing into that of remorse. Gradually, his blank stare fell to the stain on the floor, and then to the dark monitor of the television.

"So, how old are you, Grant?" Vivian called from the kitchen. "I'm not going to be in *tomorrow's* paper, am I?"

Grant frowned, his eyes growing dark and bitter. "Twenty-one," Grant sulked.

"Oh, great. I'm just a cougar. Well, *good* for me." Rummaging around in the cabinet below the kitchen sink, she pushed and pulled things aside to get every product with bleach she owned. "At least my *snatch* tastes like I'm – ow!" she screeched, hitting her head while exiting the cabinet.

She paused with a sudden rush of the memory of falling to the floor in her hallway and hitting her head.

"What's wrong with older women?"

Grant's booming voice brought her back into the present. Blinking furiously, she groaned, carefully proceeding to exit the cabinet before standing up with a handle full of chemicals.

"Who are you calling old?" she winced, making her way back towards the hall. But upon reaching the stain, she wobbled, and actually fell to her knees.

"Whoa. Easy. Stay down," he warned, as he rushed to her side.

Stay down… Stay down… Stay down. The words rang in her memory as her eyes shut tight. Struggling to open them, Vivian found herself in a dark replica of her home, and she was alone on the floor, looking up at a darkened silhouette with a broken wine bottle in its hand.

"Hey," Grant said, gently shaking her from her figment. Watching her muted expression, he gave her repeated gentle shakes, until the light once again returned to her eyes.

"What.…"

"Geez," Grant sighed as he wrapped one of his arms around her back and helped her to her feet.

Vivian was barely able to grab onto him as

they made their way to the sofa.

"You should take up a life of sobriety, if you ask me."

"Funny," Vivian exhaled as she was settled on the sofa cushion, her eyes constantly blurring into focus.

"Where're your blankets?"

"Upstairs … hallway closet."

"Think you can manage not drinking in the time it'll take me to get you one and a cup of coffee?"

"Funny," was the only thing she could manage as her head pulsed, her ears ringing from the distant sound of sirens outside.

Her eyes closed as he made the trip upstairs. Resting one palm against her forehead, her other hand reached for the remote.

Maybe I really do need to stop drinking, she thought as she turned the television back on.

"As a former investigator, it was no secret that Miss Black had crossed paths with some dangerous individuals," the reporter spoke into her microphone as she stood near a neighborhood's gated community in the late afternoon. *The sun had begun to set and the red and blue lights of nearby police cars danced across the woman's mocha face.*

"Heh," Vivian scoffed with a subtle shake of her head. "You and me both, sister."

"Having been known for her ruthless tactics in securing suspects, it's thought that after being released from her employment, Vivian may have been targeted by said individuals as a way to get back at her for locking their fellow criminals away."

Vivian's head throbbed with immense pressure after hearing the woman speak her name, and undergoing the otherworldly and displacing sensation that *she* was being spoken about. Brows furrowing, her hand clutched at her hairline as her temple ached. But even still, she increased the volume of television as the woman continued to speak, her mind racing with nowhere to go.

"Currently, no suspects have been identified, nor has the former investigator's status been confirmed. After not being seen leaving or entering her house in the past six days, neighbors informed the police of their suspicions."

"Six!" Vivian gawked, eyes wide as her head pounded.

Her hand moved to the back of her head before coming back down. But when she did, and she was startled to see her palm smeared with blood. She jerked up from the sofa and spun around to check her cushions, but there was no blood to be found. Again, she reached her hands to the back of her head and brought them to her face, whimpered when seeing the blood darken and spread.

"Receiving a warrant to search the home, police have prepared to investigate the property after attempts to contact Miss Black have gone unanswered. We await the police's discovery," the reporter stated as the camera panned to a view of Vivian's house.

"What..." Vivian began to tremble as Grant trotted back down the stairs. As his heavy feet thudded against the stairs, his face emerged from the shadows, and it all came rushing back to her.

Bringing him home with her.

The night of drinking.

Of passionate sex.

Of murder.

She remembered it all. Coming down in the middle of the night and catching him stealing from her cabinets. He drew a kitchen knife on her, and she broke an empty bottle of wine on the end table in the hallway to defend herself. They'd struggled, weapons scattering on the floor. Both of them had gotten a number of stabs in, but it was the blow to Vivian's head that knocked her unconscious, and she bled out over several minutes.

She hadn't hit her head. *He had bashed it in.*

That wasn't a wine stain on her floor. *It was blood. Her blood.*

"*You*," Vivian snarled, voice trembling.

Grant stopped as he reached the last step, and just before the police kicked in her front door, flooding the room with flashlights, trampling feet, and men in uniform. Suddenly, her view of her house changed. The lights were off, allowing the cop's flashlights shine in both of their eyes. Vivian flinched away from the light, while Grant stared her down. But when Vivian looked towards the entering group again, she gasped, her bloody hand clamping over her mouth when seeing the lights flicker over her dead body, now visible over the gruesome blood stain in the hallway. Body limb, eyes wide and blank.

"… Oh my god. *Oh my god*," Vivian wept hysterically.

"That's her," one of the men confirmed on his radio. "Call it in!" he shouted to the coroner on duty, calling him in as the lights were turned on.

Grant stared grimly at the body as the group dispersed to place markers all over the house. One beside the broken wine bottle. One beside the kitchen knife. One beside the body. Flashes from surrounding cameras filled the room as Vivian launched herself in Grant's direction. The room spun, along with her stomach as her mind feebly attempted to wrap around the reality that was being made painfully clear. Dropping the nonexistent blanket on the floor, Grant flinched to catch her balled fists as she threw them at him.

"Bastard! I'll kill you!" Vivian screamed.

"Gonna be hard to do," Grant grimaced as he fought to restrain her.

"Got another body back here, sir!" one of the officers shouted from the backyard, having gone out from the back door in the kitchen. "Stab wounds consistent with both the knife and wine bottle."

The commanding officer sighed as he removed his protective helmet. "Took the son of a bitch out with you, huh?"

"Why?" Vivian cried, continuously trying to hit against Grant's chest. "Why, you son of a –"

"I wasn't going to kill you!" Grant hollered in

defense.

"Liar!"

"I was just going to steal some silverware. But you came down and started attacking me! I was defending myself!"

"Aren't you the fucking wolf in sheep's clothing?" she spat.

"You wouldn't stop," Grant grimaced, his grip loosening in genuine remorse. "I'm ..."

Vivian paused, thrown off by the displaced look of sorrow engraved in his dark expression.

"I'm sorry."

Vivian exhaled in an anguished whine of refusal, pushing away from him and turning around in time to see the tarp go over her body, her knees buckling and landing her on the floor a moment later.

"I'm so sorry."

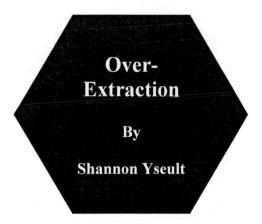

Over-Extraction

By

Shannon Yseult

"I shouldn't be here," Erin says aloud, while looking out the car window at Heather's two-story white house. The windows are dark. *Is the stalker gone? Should she go in?*

Heather's quivering voice-message replays in her head. *"I think someone is following me. Erin, I'm scared. I need you to watch the house tonight. I know you shouldn't, but it would make me feel better knowing you were there — in*

case he tries to do more than watch."

She dries her palms on her pants, fingers brushing against the cold metal flashlight hooked to her duty belt.

Heather might be lying to get Erin to show up at her house. She is that manipulative. Their failed relationship full of examples proving it.

Yet the tremble in Heather's voice reveals so much. The social, independent, strong woman that she had fallen in love with, and loved hard and long enough to marry, never had anything but confidence in her voice, never a second guess in her head. While it had been a wonder to love, it was also the doom of the relationship.

By the sound of her voice, Heather must think there is a real danger, perhaps even more than she could overcome by herself. Erin curses under her breath, knowing that she should tell another police officer about the situation, call in some backup, at least tell her partner. But then she would have to admit that she had been in contact with Heather. That fucking restraining order was half of the problem. The other half was the looks she would get when walking past the desks in the morning. They barely hid their current impressions about Erin, particularly after the last incident.

Erin looks over the house again. The fence guarded garden sprouts, made visible by solar-powered lights Erin installed years ago. The same day she had changed the locks on the doors. Her key now lives under the ashtray of her rust-covered blue car. She'd thought about giving it back, a symbol of the true end of their relationship, yet she can't bring herself to do something so finalizing. They had been so happy together, or Erin had thought.

The scene replays in her head as it had so many sleepless nights before. Opening the door and placing a bag of Mexican food from their favorite restaurant on the table. Hearing a scream. Running upstairs, those never-ending stairs. Finding the door to the bedroom open and Heather on top of that man.

Heather's words come, unwelcome, from the depths. *"Babe, you can't be jealous. He's helping me with a little physical attention, attention you can't give me." She put her hand on Erin's shoulder, her other hand holding her silk robe to her body. Erin jerks away from the touch. A shudder spread through her body, meeting her face, filling her with the single emotion of loss. Loss covered in tears.*

She doesn't remember much more than screams filling the air, a puddle of tears forming at her feet, and her emotions leaving her as a cold, empty shell.

Finances forced her to stay in the house. Her name was next to Heather's on the mortgage and the divorce took over a year. No one could handle mortgage and rent payments for that long.   The key's presence pulled at her. All of the feelings locked in the key living under the ash tray. The end of the relationship, the trials in the divorce, Erin surviving it all—

—a movement down the street.

Erin puts her hand on her gun, squinting down the moonlit road. She sees a cat walk out from under a car. Erin lets out a sigh, leaning back in the seat. *This whole situation is bad.* She takes her hand off of the gun and picks up her thermos of coffee, taking the lid off. The smell fills the car and the steam warms her face. She pours a cup and puts the thermos away.

Taking a sip of the dark and bitter brew, she once again considers calling for backup. It would be easier to watch the house and there would be a record of the incident if anything bad happened now, or in the future.

But would they even believe her? She is the one with a restraining order, the one they know isn't supposed to be here. If she doesn't have a name to give them, a suspect, then they'd just write her up and ignore the problem, maybe sign her up for another couple of weeks with the counselor. Her small hands grip the flimsy, white cup, too tight, making it bend.

A light goes on in the house. The master bedroom.

No one had come or gone since that cat. Even with the lack of streetlights she trusts herself that much. *Maybe Heather is getting a glass of water. She does that late at night, particularly if she's been drinking.*

Erin holds her breath as she watches the curtain-obscured window. Would Heather look and see that she was there?

She decides to count. It should take Heather less than twenty seconds to get to the bathroom, get a glass of water, and walk back to the bed.

Eighteen...

Nineteen...

Twenty...

Twenty-one...

Twenty-two...

Erin puts her coffee down, wiping her palms on her pants again. Maybe she's using the bathroom too. A couple more seconds wouldn't hurt. Unless the stalker is in the bathroom.

There was no sign of that. It should be fine. Everything should be fine. Erin takes a deep breath. She doesn't need her therapist here to tell her she is high-strung and anxious. If she could get herself back in control she would make better decisions.

"Damn," she hisses, slamming her hand on the rim of the steering wheel. Why did this have to happen now? Busting drug dens and flashy car chases don't raise her blood pressure like this. One message from Heather and here she is, having an anxiety attack.

Fifty-three...

Fifty-four...

Fifty-five.

Erin takes the key out from under the ashtray, spilling a few coins on the floor. She keeps an eye on the bedroom window where a shadow passes. Erin puts her hand on the door handle as a gunshot splits the air.

Dark and Bitter

Being Colette

By

Shan Jeniah Burton

Colette's shriek ricochets in my head, and I spin to check on her, my heartbeat echoing the thunder that shakes the cabin. I barely hop backward in time to keep the log from landing on my toes.

"Are you all right?" She's hugging her quilt tight, hands fisted in the patchwork fabric. Her eyes are wide, and she looks like a terrified little girl. I want to go to her side, but something keeps my feet planted. "Are you c-cold, C-Colette?"

"It just scared me. It's silly, I know." She shrugs a little, frowning, and the child-Colette vanishes like melting ice. Finally, I manage to take a step closer, then another, as she keeps talking. "Did I ever tell you there was a storm the day before my ninth birthday? Thunder right over the house, shaking it, just like tonight. I thought I was going to die."

"Don't talk about dying!" It hisses out, sounding harsher than the storm. I don't want to talk to Colette this way.

"Hey, come here, Mister Fly." The set of her chin warns me not to argue. I kneel by her chaise lounge. "I obviously didn't die. I got to open my presents. I had my chocolate cake and mint chocolate chip ice cream."

"But you don't even like ice cream, Colette." Why are we talking about dessert, as though this is just another night at home?

"I loved it both back then, and mint chocolate chip was my favorite." Her arms snake out from under the pile of quilts to pull me into her web. Her grass-green eyes are intent, their flecks of gold shimmering in the firelight. "Last night, you would have laughed at that story. And if you heard thundersnow, you'd have danced me out to the porch to listen, even if I didn't really want to go." She strokes fingers through my hair and across my forehead. Her touch is warm and alive. "And when I said it was too cold, you'd carry me back in, and we'd be lucky to get the door closed before you showed me just how excited you are by winter weather." She smiles softly, but I see shadows in her eyes. "What's wrong tonight, my love?"

"You know what's wrong. And you haven't told me if you're still c-cold." Why do I stammer every time I say that word?

"Come find out for yourself." She lifts the covers a little, tipping her head the way she always does when she wants me. She figured out right away that it usually distracts me from everything else. But it's not going to work tonight.

I snug the blankets around her instead, trying to ignore the way the back of my hand grazes her breast. "The doctor said you need to take it easy for a few days. So just tell me if you're warm enough."

"Just because you come into my web doesn't mean I'm going to pounce on you, Mister Fly." She catches my hand and nibbles on my fingers. When she plays spider, she doesn't hide her spinnerets, and I'm lousy at resisting her. The truth is, I usually don't even try.

But tonight is different.

I reclaim my hand, and go back to restocking the woodpile. I'm going to make damned sure it stays nice and toasty in here.

Not like the dark and bitter waters of the lake. I'd had the whole day planned, right down to the last detail, and then my buddies invited us on that last-minute ice-fishing trip.

Colette didn't want to go. She said the ice wasn't safe, and we should stay warm inside instead of being outside with a storm coming. But I convinced her, and we went.

I should have listened to her.

She's quiet now, spinning her webs. Even though she doesn't say or do anything, I can feel her weaving. Invisible silken threads tighten around me in a lover's embrace. I've got to resist, no matter how hard it is, at least until I'm convinced she's really all right. I'm going to be sure there's plenty of wood to keep my Colette warm, because the storm is expected to rage through tomorrow.

By tomorrow night, the lake ice is going to be a foot thick.

Stop thinking about that. Tend to the fire. Make sure she's warm, and doesn't exert herself. Don't think about the ice, or the sound of it cracking.

I back away from that thought. We're here, now, and safe. The tiny velvet box is heavy in my pocket. First things first, though. I keep busy with the stacking. Back and forth; back and forth. The rhythm is comforting, and Colette looks like she's drowsy and warm, just the way I want her.

"You've got enough firewood there for half a lifetime." It's a sleepy purr.

"Don't want to run out in the storm." Thunder rumbles again, further off this time. I don't turn around. I'm a little afraid she's not truly here. But then something caresses my backside. I turn to glare sternly at the unrepentant foot poking out from under the sheltering quilts. "You're supposed to stay bundled up. Doctor's orders."

"You're kidding, right? You're making a bonfire already; add any more wood, and you might burn the place down. That would be way *too* hot. Put those logs down, Mister Fly, and come hold me. Nothing warms me up better than you do." She lifts the blanket again, revealing her bared breast.

I realize I'm caressing papery birch bark, and know I'm lost. Her webs always get me all wrapped up. I turn and put the logs on the pile, and I don't need to see her to know she's smiling. I kneel beside her again, reaching for the soft flesh she's displaying, then pull my hand back before finally giving in to the inevitable. Like a fly, I'm caught. Miss Spider licks her lips.

Her lips were blue, this afternoon. *Her green eyes panicked. Her skin white and cold. So cold.*

"Colette, you almost..." Her lips claim mine hungrily. Pink. Not blue. Not freezing into an unvoiced cry. She smothers my words, but she can't erase my memories. When she lets me loose, I stare into her eyes and finish the thought.

"You damn near died."

"And yet, I'm right here." Miss Spider isn't done with me yet; she covers my hand with hers, and moves it over her breast. "Feel how much I want you, love you, need you." She arches into my touch. She is mine. I'm absolutely hers.

Isn't that all that matters?

Colette wriggles over a little, making room for me on the chaise, and lifts the blanket more. She thinks she has me ensnared, but I tuck her in again. She pouts, but doesn't try to keep me there. A spider can afford to wait. "Don't put any more logs on that fire, if you expect to keep me under all these layers." She stirs, and I look away before she can tempt me further. She refuses to wear a robe, and whatever's left of my resistance will go up in flames if I see any more of her skin bared to the dancing shadows and glowing firelight. I search for a distraction, and notice the coffee I left on the side table this morning. I don't really want it, but it's something to occupy my mouth and hands. I take a swig and spit it back into the mug.

"What's wrong?"

"It's so old, it's gone bitter."

"I'll get you more." She moves restlessly. She's never been very patient with being fussed over. Not even after this afternoon.

"Forget it." I say it as if forgetting is easy. But it's not.

I want to forget, but I can't. *Lying flat on the ice to spread out my weight. The rope cutting into my hips.*

Reaching down, and down. Catching her upstretched hands. Shivering. "Can't let go…" Her face, panicking, mouth open into an "O." Dark and bitter water flowing into her, drowning her voice. Her frozen hands clutching mine. My frantic yelling at whoever's got the other end of the rope. "Pull us back. Pull her out! Hurry! Hurry!"

I need to be sure she's actually here, and alive. I put the mug down and climb onto the lounge with her. She smiles and wraps a quilt around me, like a web. But even flies sometimes get free. I had a plan for tonight, before the water. I shudder, and she tries to pull me over on top of her. But I'm not going to let her distract me yet.

"Colette. My Colette. I'm so sorry! I shouldn't have badgered you to come. I should have told the guys we had other plans."

"Shhh. You said tonight was going to be all about me, and I don't want to talk about it. I don't want to *talk* at all." She wriggles half on top of me, and I don't argue. I did promise her tonight. We'll go nice and slow, once I take care of this one bit of business.

"It *is* your night. All night. But there's something I've got to do first, before I give myself over to you, Miss Spider." I reach into my pocket and wrap my hand around the velvet box. "Colette, I really shouldn't have made you go with me today."

"You didn't force me to come. And it wasn't you who drove that truck over thin ice. Now, let's stop talking."

"I've got one more question for you, Miss Spider." I take a deep breath and pull out the box. My fingers tremble so much, I'm sure I'm going to drop it. I manage to get it open, hold it so the stone catches the firelight and reflects it in Miss Spider's gleaming green eyes. Her lips form a little "oh." I squeeze my own eyes closed, and open them again. She's grinning expectantly now, even bouncing a little.

"Will you allow me the honor and delight of being yours, Colette? Being your husband f-f-for the r-rest of our l-lives?" The words tangle and stutter out of my throat. *Why am I stammering again?*

But her smile just gets wider, like she doesn't even notice me tripping over my own tongue. "You want to be my Mister Spider? And for me to be your Missus Fly?"

"W-will y-you?"

"Always, always, always, my love."

I slip the ring on her finger. She takes my hand in her newly decorated one. She moves them together to a place that leaves no doubt what she wants. I'm in her web for good now. I let go of all resistance, all the memories from this afternoon, and give myself to Colette.

Much later, I drift toward sleep with Colette's warm bare body draped over me.

Ice cutting and numbing my cheek, dark and bitter water lapping against the jagged edge. Her hands cold and lifeless in my grip. She stares up from below, her mouth a frozen, panicked "oh."

Her hands slip out of mine. She's sinking. Down and away, into the freezing waters of the lake.

I scramble after her. But something yanks me back. I'm sliding along the ice, further and further from my Colette…

The thundersnow soundtrack plays on, and I lay awake, treasuring these peaceful moments. *Just this once, let him sleep through the night, with me. Let him wake up and want me, not his precious dead Colette.*

The lighting effects flash through the room, and his hand clenches on my breast, a painful warning of what's next. The soundtrack follows up with another percussive thunderclap. The walls and floor shake.

"C-Colette! C-Colette!" He sits straight up, and embers glint in his unseeing eyes. "C-Colette!"

"I'm here. I'm here." I whisper the same thing, again and again, until he sags back into my arms, sleeping peacefully once more. I savor his nearness, his solid weight against me, his scent, the way the firelight dances on his warm skin.

I want to stay here forever.

I want this to be real.

I listen to the recorded storm, wishing I could believe in this reality the way he does. But that's not why I'm here.

He's still sleeping soundly when I extricate myself. I don't hurry. There's a lulling quality to the waning fire, the deep breaths of the sleeping man, the way the shifting light emphasizes the generous sprinkling of silver in hair that had been solidly black when I first came to him.

"Colette...." He murmurs softly, but doesn't stir. I fight the urge to ignore my script, and crawl back under the covers beside him. But I've fought this battle before. If I don't leave when I'm supposed to, I won't be allowed to see him again.

"My Colette....my bride...."

The fingers of my right hand go to the fourth finger of the left. I caress the ring for a moment. Then I slip it off, tipping it until the engraving catches the light. The room is too dim to read it, but the words are carved in my heart: "*My Colette – Always, always, always,*" and the date.

Today's date - if today was eleven years ago.

I sigh, and the sleeping man echoes it. I kneel where he knelt, and reach under the chaise, groping until my fingers strike something small and hard. I get hold of it stealthily, watching him the whole time. If he wakes, I must still be Colette for him.

I finagle the ring back into the box as I watch him. He's on his stomach, shoulders rising and falling evenly, slightly shaggy hair tousled from our lovemaking. I long to climb back into the warmth of the nest, drag my fingers through the sensual resistance of his curls, and make love to him again.... and this time, maybe he'd want *me*, the way he still wants Colette.

I look for a reason to stay. *Just a little longer.* I

gulp the rest of his old coffee. It tastes like a truth I don't want to face.

He loves Colette, who is dead. I'm alive, and I love him. But he doesn't know me as myself, only as Colette.

I watch him sleep, imagining I'm free to sprinkle kisses over his shoulder, taste the sweat on his warm flushed skin.

The soundtrack reaches the point where the thunder eases to soft distant growls.

Please, not yet!

But there's no protest I dare voice aloud.

I kiss my fingers and brush them over his shoulder. It's a poor substitute. I bite my lip to keep from crying. The dark and bitter dregs that coat my tongue make me think of the waters that swallowed his Colette. The aftertaste lingers as I back my way out the door.

I stand there in the doorway for a long and dangerous moment, tempted to go back, pretend he's mine, and I'm his. The tears bite the back of my throat, blending with the acrid flavors of two loves that can never be requited.

Dark and Bitter

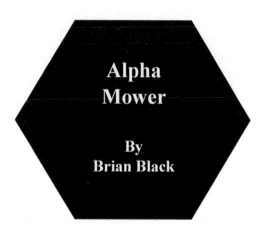

"*Identity: AAR 4500-SPM Self-Programming Module, fully Artificially Capable Lawn Care Agent. Power up initiated. Full logging set to on: Verbose mode. Time and date stamp: Friday, July 24th, 2054, Time: 0700.*"

"*Begin systems diagnostics: All systems normal at 100%. Bearing greasing procedure begun. Wheels greased. Mower blade bearings greased. Standard maintenance completed.*"

"Secondary systems check begin: Electrical deterrent rod 25%, 50%, 75%, 100% power. Check completed. All power levels available. AI subsystems check: random routine implementation complete. Instantiation of random self-programming successful. Self-Programming online and active."

"Sensor systems check begin: Visual. Tracking outdoor movement. Targeting and tracking of one, two, three separate objects within range. Visual tracking system active. Heat mode: Module not installed. Check failed. Infrared mode: Module not installed. Check failed. Microphone check: 30, 35, 33, 33 decibels. Microphone active and functional. Touch sensors check: Three found. Touch sensors active and functional."

"Last checks…"

. . .

. . .

"Complete. All systems online and active. Startup log complete."

"Begin daily tasks. Current task list: Mow current local area. Begin."

"Visual search protocol for local lawns initiated. Ten meters. Negative. Twenty meters. Negative. Thirty. Forty. Fifty. Negative. Search initiated."

A small flat dark-red object rolled smoothly out of a garage. It was beat up, dented, and unevenly colored, as if it had been painted by hand, only where some previous accident was. An electronic whir emanated from it every few seconds as it took in its local environment.

"Begin environment assessment."

"Temperature: Seventy-two degrees Fahrenheit."

"Weather: Fair; Light winds, East, five mph."

"Moving objects detected in visual range: Zero."

"Number of sounds in proximity: Zero."

"Last task target in proximity: 847 meters, Southeast, Label : Front lawn."

It paused for a moment, verifying its reading, and began moving toward the front lawn.

The sky had an ominous abnormal haze to it: part orange, part gray. The mower rolled past the scorched barn where three dozen cattle lay rotting amid flies buzzing wildly. Part of the roof was caved in and the structure seemed jolted. Unsound, in a word. All in-progress searches for lawn failed. What remained was warped, brown, and decrepit. The mower slowly panned a corn field with smoke billowing up from it in the distance.

Towards the edge of the property the power-lines and poles were toppled over. Sparks were still coming off the power-coupler on the electronic fence, which normally curtailed the range of the automated devices on the farm. The mower sent out continual pings and waited to receive a response to know the bounds of the property. None were found and the mower moved on, over the scorched hill and past the patch of forest blown over by some monstrous force. Search protocols continued with no response.

The mower carried on over the hill, giving way to a view overlooking the nearby city. Thick, black smoke came up from the buildings. A few looked as if some deity had smacked them with a sledgehammer; leaving them windowless, lurching, crippled.

The roadways were cluttered with cars everywhere, even on highway dividers. Some were on their sides or tops. A few were resting on their rear bumpers, nearly vertical, after sliding down a hill. All cars remained in place, suspended in time, lifeless. As the mower moved down the shallow hill in the direction of the city, more vehicles came into view. If the heat sensor had been installed, it would've registered that some of the vehicles were on fire. Without it, they were registered as random obstacles.

The sky was buzzing with small, nondescript drones. They littered the sky, conducting surveillance, reconnaissance, and tracking the signals from the now-standard implants everyone was injected with at birth. All these drones flew about, reading and transmitting data to and fro into an ever-present electronic soup.

The mower paused and read the input it was getting.

"Begin environment assessment."

"Moving objects detected in visual range: Error. Overflow; Ten plus detected; Source: Aerial."

"Number of sounds in proximity : Error. Overflow; Ten plus detected sounds; Source: Aerial."

"Additional Information: 10+ satellite signals present."

"Path-tracking: Obstacles present, creating map."

It registered the movement, constructed a

digital grid in memory of the local obstacles, and carried on.

The mower moved past a car with the door hanging open, a rotting body hanging out of it, mouth open, flesh burnt off and charred. A blackened rotting hand was still clutching the steering wheel, the person's attempt to escape the blast radius obviously futile. Flies swarmed around it in a black cloud. Cockroaches, thrilled at their new windfall, scurried for cover as the mower passed by. A small drone wavered above, attempting to read data from the chip in the dead body.

Sensors fired at full capacity, bringing back no readings of lawn anywhere in the vicinity. The mower moved towards the highway divider, easily slipping under the guard rail, and on to the other side. The sensors showed movement.

Off in the distance an automated vehicle sped quickly through the area, traversing past the clutter of cars, moving them out of the way as it approached. Behind it was a long convoy of more automated vehicles, waiting to get past. The mower stopped briefly to calculate the trajectory and speed needed to cross the road.

"Begin environment assessment."

"Moving objects detected in visual range, more than ten; Source, Terrestrial."

"Identify: Road-clearing vehicle; Mercedes XLP-40 'Sweeper'."

The mower's hard-drive clattered while it processed the data.

"Other object's identities cannot be determined."

The Sweeper was bearing down on the mower's position at a moderate clip. The mower began calculating the wheel spin rate versus the distance from the oncoming vehicle, factoring the Sweeper's rate of speed. The calculations were returned and a glowing red negative number blinked on the mower's internal display. The spin rate was far below the speed needed to pass through the area safely. The mower's internal protocols were reported.

"Protocol One: Survive."

"Protocol Two: Mow."

"Protocol Three: Seek Repair."

The mower tagged the current action in its log under Protocol One, hurriedly altered the code responsible for the wheel spin rate, and set it beyond the internal safety limits. A red warning light appeared in its internal display. The Sweeper was nearly on top of the mower with a full head of steam, gaining ground very quickly. The mower moved at full speed, aided by the new routine, wheels spinning in the process.

The Sweeper passed by just as the mower slipped under a car, picking up the vehicle and pushing it out of the way, knocking a body out of the smashed car window as it did. The wheel of the moved car banged the top of the mower as it passed, knocking it back into the road. The mower spun its wheels again and moved at full tilt out of the way, just in time to avoid being run over as automated vehicles filed obediently behind the Sweeper in a seemingly endless procession.

On the other side of the highway the mower picked up readings of lawn and activated mowing procedures as per Protocol Two. Automated vehicles were still moving by ceaselessly in the background. A drone overhead took particular interest in the scene and the mower specifically, its red recording light blinking. After a moment, it paused, recording light off, its data processing, and then it rapidly disappeared into the distance toward the city.

Having finished its current task, the mower switched back to search mode and rolled on from the highway area. It began to advance down a sloped embankment bordering the highway and started calculating the braking capabilities versus the slope of the hill. Calculations came back positive and the mower proceeded.

The mower went over a section of loose rubble, which cracked and gave way after it passed. A few pebbles started cascading down the slope, followed by larger pieces of asphalt, escalating into a shower of rocks and debris raining down onto the mower, knocking it a distance down the hill. *"Braking procedures activated."* Unintended movement abated. The mower paused until the landslide subsided.

The mower began, moving slowly again, when another landslide, this one larger than the first, shifted the entire section of soil the mower was driving over, sending it tumbling down the hill. Alarms went off on the mower's display. It activated braking procedures again, this time to no avail. Calculations came back negative repeatedly. The mower spun its wheels in the opposite direction of its trajectory with no effect. Sensors indicated a significant height drop in the direction the mower was headed. The mower activated a rake attachment, springing out of its side, to slow the rate of descent, internally logged under Protocol One, and dug it deeply into the shifting ground. Rate of descent slowed slightly, but the calculations and alarms were still displayed.

A peppered mix of mostly soil and one part mower fell off the overpass and crashed onto the ground below, dropping the mower directly on one of its wheels with dirt continuing to rain down on top of it. A dusty haze filled the air as the avalanche of rock and dirt wound down.

Another alert went off, this time signifying damage. Diagnostics began and the wheel gyro it landed on flagged as damaged. Protocol Three kicked in, *"Seek Repair."*

It began testing the wheel to determine if it could withstand further use without suffering additional damage, *"Twenty-percent speed capable without inducing incapacity."*

The mower initiated a satellite repair request and waited for a response. 18.2 seconds later a response came back: *"Repair station 248, six-point-seven miles away. GPS coordinates sent, station standing by."*

The mower started down the service road at the current maximum speed, with 3.35 hours ETA. It set a course along main roads to ensure optimal speed to the station.

After nearly a half mile down, the fractured service road opened out onto local main roads. Telephone and power poles were laying in the roads, some sparking manically. The mower processed the random movement of a power line in the road jumping like a child on a sugar high, predicted its future movement, and plotted a course around it. It passed around a number of downed street signs, bent and warped, reflective paint melted off.

The town was piercingly silent. Only the occasional screech from a vulture overhead, circling in the sky, or a drone languidly buzzing past while tracking various data, punctuated the dead quiet. Local buildings' windows were nonexistent, blasted out completely. A number of buildings were shifted, cracked, and crumbling, once beautiful and stoic, now pounded and shattered. Random bits of bricks and other debris were scattered in the street. Some dark imprints on the building faces were oddly human shaped.

The mower passed by a solid-looking concrete garage with the door blown inward, leaving a gap at the bottom. An empty coffee cup blew by in the light breeze, the contents formerly dark and bitter. Just beyond, in the dim light, a number of bodies lay huddled together in the garage, rotting, burned, partially skeletal.

Glowing eyes appeared in the dark. A mangy dog emerged from under the door, teeth bared and growling, remaining neck hair raised. Patches of fur were missing and a large section of skin on its side was gone, revealing bloody ribs. The remaining fur was matted and grimy, with portions burnt. One eye was milky white and the other blood-red around the frantic distressed pupil. Blood and dangling flesh dripped from its teeth, and the fur around its mouth was dark red with saturated blood. The dog lunged at the mower, which changed course to circumvent the potential hazard. The dog continued growling until the mower was well out of view, and limped slowly back into the garage to continue feeding on the dead bodies. A drone hovered overhead filming the scene with marked interest, its hard-drive light blinking slowly.

The air was thick and hazy and faraway objects appeared indistinct. Silhouettes moved through the mist as small packs of dogs moved from building to building in the distance. The road was cracked and buckled, forcing the mower to recalculate the path it took continuously. The mower veered down an alleyway between two buildings. A wake of vultures feasting on a semi-melted corpse, nearly consumed except for the throat, leapt out of the way as the mower passed. A murder of crows were nearby, cawing madly, waiting for an opening to gain some of the spoils.

An alert popped up in the mower's display: "*Arrival at repair station T-minus one minute.*" The mower crested a small hill and arrived at the repair station, input its jack into the door lock mechanism and sent the repair request receipt code. Mechanisms beyond the door produced a heavy metallic clack, and, shortly after, the sound of gears turning madly, caused a small service door to swing up in notchy, jerky movements.

The mower drove in to the station. All lights were off and no movement was detected. The mower parked itself at the repair bay, connected into the Tesla-jack, and received the station status, *"Error, disabled."* The error code indicated damage to the station. The mower checked the current firmware to see if it could receive new programming. *"Yes."*

The mower uploaded new instructions into the station controller's ROM and requested a reboot.

"AAV Maintenance Station OS : Version 2.09"

"Station number: 248"

"Repair bays: 4"

"Repair level capable: Basic"

"Repairs possible: Standard maintenance, basic mechanical."

"Repairs offline: Detailed maintenance, advanced mechanical, mechanical upgrades, body repair."

The station waited for a request.

"*Wheel repair requested.*" The station immediately sprang to life. Mechanical arms of all sorts started swinging around and conducting the repair. A little more than an hour later, the station was finished, including standard maintenance, all arms retracting into their respective slots. The repair log indicated eighty-five percent speed capability restored. The additional fifteen percent required advanced mechanism repair.

The mower evaluated its protocols, and requested detailed GPS information from the station. The station complied, adding a series of new locations to the mower's internal maps. The mower logged the repair and exited the station.

Long-range sensors and GPS map evaluation revealed a local high school requiring standard lawncare 1.8 miles away. The mower set course at full speed.

As the mower moved into less populated areas, houses lay demolished. Walls, pieces of roof, and other debris lay everywhere with little more than an occasional piece of building left standing. Trees and power poles were snapped, bent, and broken with many branches laying in the street, forcing the mower to course-correct continuously. It passed by a series of bare foundations with lumber strewn all around them. Houses were nearly all flattened, with the few remaining ones looking mangled like a monster came along and twisted them in-hand, and dropped them back in place.

A kettle of vultures swooped through one of the blasted out windows in one of the few standing houses. Noise emanated from inside, and a few crows flew out. Sounds of an activity were picked up by the mower's microphone from inside, a squabble of some sort clearly occurring. A crow flew and landed on the ledge of the window, a finger in its mouth. Happy with its claim, it took flight to a nearby bent-over tree and began feasting.

The mower arrived at the high school and immediately set to work mowing the bits of lawn it found intact. In the background, the high school lay in ruins, the top floor shifted away from the bottom, with one portion dangling off the lower floor. There were more human-shaped shadows projected onto the side of the building, like ashen scarecrows attempting to scare away any onlooker. The mower moved around the large patches of burnt lawn, going at full capacity to locate viable lawn.

A short distance away, as the mower passed an irregular open garage port that looked intended for a motorcycle. A distinct pinpoint red light turned on in the dark of the port, slowly phasing in, and then blinking consistently. A unit nearly filling the entire opening came out and began moving toward the mower.

The mower skipped a large section of mutilated burnt lawn, continued reading the area, and moved toward the football field just beyond the building, where intact lawn was.

As the mower moved past the corner of the school, it noticed movement on its radar and a red blip became highlighted on its display. The mower began processing the radar signature and requested further information. The results came back as a large bulky unit rolled slowly into view.

The unit's side was stamped with "Middleton High School" and the serial number "JSB 1201A-P". The mower searched its database and identified the unit as a Multi-Purpose Lawncare Unit with "Protector" module upgrade.

The mower continued, monitoring the

Protector's position, which was rapidly closing on it. The mower looked up the protocols again and proceeded, as per Protocol Two: Mow. It mowed the football field, bordered by contorted bleachers, broken lights, and a leaning scoreboard.

Once the mower started, the sound of lawnmower blades punctuating the air, the Protector stepped up its pursuit and raced towards the field. The mower continued its task, still noting the movement of the unit, very nearly to it.

The Protector moved onto the field, directly pursuing the mower, a small hatch sliding open on top of it.

A small box popped up from the hatch, arcs of purple spark racing around it.

The mower tracked the position of the Protector. "*Initiate defensive mode. Begin Tier-One evasive tactics. Bring armament online.*" It flipped a large cattle prod attachment out of its frame, and charged it to full power, blue sparks leaping off the end.

The Protector charged its electrolaser to fifty percent and aggressively pursued to intercept the intruder. The mower retreated away from the Protector, hampered by its limited speed, with the

Protector closing quickly.

The Protector closed in and the electrolaser fired huge blinding arcs of purple lightning. One of the arcs contacted the mower briefly, bolts of electricity dancing around the frame, leaving a black singe mark and causing a power surge. The mower's power dipped momentarily, the light on top dimming and flickering, but internal protection circuits prevented a full shutdown.

The mower deactivated mowing and fled at full speed.

The Protector, satisfied with having deterred the intruder, ceased its pursuit and headed off, going back to its normal guard and lawncare duties.

Just out of range, the mower began mowing again. The Protector's microphone pinged with the sound of mowing, reactivating its guard routines, and pursued full-speed, this time having powered the electrolaser up to seventy percent. Electricity pumped out of it and lightning shot from the top like a palm tree blowing in a hurricane.

The mower's sensors picked up the incoming adversary for the second time, and evasive tactics were reengaged. The mower started for the bleachers, attempting to draw the Protector in that direction.

The Protector, activating its maximum-aggression setting, "Vendetta-mode", pursued bellicosely. The mower scrambled under the bleachers with the Protector closing fast. The mower reactivated mowing under the bleachers, which made a light on the Protector flash and then flicker rapidly, a mechanical howl screaming from its speakers.

The Protector's tactical evaluation routines returned the conclusion: It's being mocked, provoked, and incited. The Protector initiated a sweep of the area, revealing no humans in the vicinity, and deactivated safety precautions. Electrolaser powered up to eighty-five percent.

The blip for the mower moved off the Protector's radar screen. Tracking switched exclusively to auditory through the microphone. The sound of mowing continued under the bleachers. Pursuit continued.

The mower stopped with the blades still going, waiting for the Protector to get closer. The mower calculated the interception time to be twenty-four seconds.

At twenty seconds, the mower prepared itself

to move as quickly as current hardware repairs allowed. Other than the lawnmower blades, there was dead silence.

Twenty-four seconds elapsed and there was still no sign of the Protector.

The mower waited another four seconds, then AI routines reevaluated the situation. *"Conclusion: Strategy failed, new plan construction necessary."* The mower scuttled towards the other end of the bleacher, turned off mowing and shifted processor priority to the microphone. Again, nothing.

The mower neared the opening out of the bleachers, moving from dark into the light of day. A looming silhouette slid into view, blocking the light at the end of the bleacher. *"Identification: Protector."*

While in motion the mower calculated its position and realized it was cut off from egress.

The result of the calculations also revealed that at the distance and close-rate of the Protector, the mower would not be able to escape by doubling back at its current maximum speed.

The mower immediately overrode the wheel-spin-rate safety limits reengaged from the repair, turned them off, and started back in the direction it came from as fast as it could, the damaged wheel gear making a hideous clicking noise. The Protector pushed power to its electrolaser as it pursued under the bleachers, bathing the scene in a purple light. Pulses of lightning flashed brilliantly and made horrible scathing roars as the electricity fractured the air molecules.

The Protector opened fire. Lightning filled the area completely, flashing the pitch-dark as bright as daylight. The electricity connected with the bleachers, and was completely sucked into them, making them glow white and then red, dissipating after the arcs did their wicked dance.

The Protector powered the electrolaser up to one-hundred percent and unleashed it again. The electricity arced wildly, angry and vicious, *everywhere*. The huge arcs caught the bleachers again, setting part of them on fire as the metal turned molten, making them creak and sag. The intensity was enough to reach the mower, still attempting to escape, and shut it down with a thud and a whir. Another arc cartwheeled back through the bleachers and hit the Protector. It shuddered in place as the power overloaded its circuits, and heaved to a stop.

Both units were now powered down, shells partially melted, scorched and smoking. The Protector had sparks shooting out of it from an access panel on its side. Lightning was still rippling through the bleachers, moshing a crazed jig.

A light on the mower blinked. It attempted to power itself on, encountering corrupted system files. *"System error 59722: System file 'Bootmgr.sys' invalid. Reset to recreate."* Power up began again. And again. A number of errors were logged on boot-up, some systems being damaged and offline. The mower reviewed the previous log files, the tail end of which was a jumble of letters, numbers, and symbols, unable to be read or processed.

The mower gleaned the current situation from the remnants of the log file, swept the radar, took stock of the immediate vicinity and visually observed the Protector, also working to power itself back on, trying to bypass the flood of errors it received each time it attempted a reboot. *"System error 29821: Central core input overload. Bypass? Y/N?"*

The mower still immobile, initiated full strategy calculation as it brought the wheel movement back online. *"Protocol One: Survive."*

The wheel routine was corrupted, *recreated*, and the mower bolted immediately out of the bleachers, wheel clacking rhythmically, towards the fencing at the edge of the field.

The Protector now moved slowly, like a bear waking from a long hibernation, in slow jolts, and then in one fluid movement, where it took up its pursuit again.

The mower exited the bleachers with the Protector tailing not far behind. The Protector fired the electrolaser again, catching the fence and grazing the mower. The fence turned cherry red and melted into a twisted hunk. The mower faltered, then continued, catching only a glancing fragment of the electricity.

The electrical arcs jumped to every metal surface nearby including the Protector, its infrared sight sensor blowing out in an audible 'pop'.

The mower launched a few feet and then powered down again, smoke rolling off its frame. It lurched a few times, trying to power back on. A large pause, a quick jerk, and then it slowly moved again.

The mower vectored itself toward the announcers booth nearby where it detected long grass where it could hide.

The Protector was jerking back and forth, attempting to make sense of its surroundings without an infrared view to rely on. Its internal view was just snow. The Protector attempted to power up the IR sensor again, but kept receiving an error message indicating damage. The third attempt produced the alternative to prioritize the microphone input. The Protector turned it on, and rerouted the input into the visual unit, creating a low-grade sonar.

The Protector picked up movement under the scoreboard and fired madly. Something tore out of the grass and the Protector blasted hard at the sound again. The fried hulk of a now-dead rabbit was launched into the air and fell down flaming.

The Protector disengaged the visual unit entirely, relying solely on the microphone. It caught hint of another sound and propelled itself in that direction, unleashing the electrolaser at it.

The tilted scoreboard lit up brightly from the sudden influx of power, the last score displayed; Home-team advantage, fifteen-to-two.

The mower's wheel was malfunctioning, now skipping more than it moved. It stopped for a moment, wheel gyro activating frantically. Any attempts to move itself proved futile and unproductive.

The Protector, having stopped to detect discernible audio, picked up a twenty-eight decibel sound from above. The Protector searched for the sound in its database and identified it as a vulture cry.

The entry on the list of sound sources was checked off and the Protector processed the rest of the list. It picked up a high-frequency whine of a wheel gyro, set an intercept vector, and catapulted in the direction of it.

The mower reviewed the recent attempts to move its damaged wheel and took its last possible approach to rectify it. It greased the wheel thoroughly and moved it in one direction, then another to work the grease through the mechanisms. The wheel at first moved jerkily, and after a few revolutions in each direction, smoothly, with an occasional click.

The Protector heaved towards it with a mechanical growl coming from its speakers. The mower picked up the Protector and propelled itself as fast as the wheel allowed once the Protector was in range, reviewing its strategy as it did.

The electrolaser wound up again, letting off a high-pitched whine as it charged, electricity leaping off the box. The Protector computed the range of the audio source, and got ready to fire again.

The Protector closely monitored the range between it and the mower. *"Range: 7.4. Close-rate: 0.5 meters per second. Ideal fire range: 2 meters."*

The mower neared one of the stadium light poles, stopping behind its base, twitching its wheel.

The Protector picked up the gyro sound above the background noise, and savagely continued pursuit. The mower, aware of the Protector's range, repeatedly fired its cattle prod at the casing of the power wire for the light cluster.

"Range: 4.1 meters."

The mower fired at the wire. Again. And again. And again. Again, again, again!

"Range: 3.5 meters."

Closing fast.

The mower moved off, slowly away from the light cluster.

"Range: 2.6 meters."

"Range: 2.1 meters."

"Range: 1.9 meters."

The Protector fired at one-hundred percent power, the *"Out-of-range"* alert still fading off its internal view. The lights on the cluster powered for an instant in a blinding flash, like the flash of a nuclear explosion, with the remaining bulbs exploding, and then rapidly dimmed. The electrical arcs moved all over the pole and then in one loud crash surged back through the electrical system, racing through the wire under the Protector, and finally launched out through the newly melted hole in the wiring. Brilliant sparks and blue lightning exploded from the junction boxes and wire in every possible direction.

The Protector twitched violently as a blanket of purple and blue electrical arcs danced all over it in a frenzy, triggering a series of loud pops, sparks, and small explosions internally. Service panels blew off and flames leapt out of the Protector as the electricity ravaged its systems.

The mower attempted to move away but a series of pulsing electrical arcs jumped from the pole to its frame, savaging its systems repeatedly in the frenzied electrical field, causing the mower to vibrate energetically.

Both units were shut down, the grass around them smoking, melted, and greasy. The light pole was blackened and sparks continued to jump out of the hole in the melted wire with an audible zap.

The field was filled with thick smoke and two smoldering hulks sat immobile. One was hideously melted and warped, sparking nonstop, on fire. The other was also melted, smoke pouring off the frame.

A few minutes passed and one twitched randomly and periodically. The twitches became more pronounced, steadily ramping up in intensity. It output a series of errors and a jumble of random characters on its display. Eventually a full power up procedure activated. Internal tests began...

The mower's groggy movement eventually became less lethargic and more consistent. It performed a system test: *"Significant damage. Review protocols."*

"Protocol One: Survive."
"Protocol Two: Mow."
"Protocol Three: Seek Repair."

The mower sent out a repair request and a

nearby location responded with GPS coordinates. The mower rolled forward, and visually inspected the Protector. "*No movement. Deactivated.*"

A diagnostic on the mowing systems came back: "*Functional; Operating within normal parameters.*" With the repair request blinking on its internal display, the mower took stock of the immediate vicinity, and entire grass field surrounding it.

The mower disregarded the immediacy of the repair, leaving a repair station waiting in the wings, as it took to earnestly mowing the large field, smoke lifting in the air, a demolished school just beyond it, vultures circling in the air.

A solitary sound emanated from the area. That was, the sound of mowing.

A Summer's Night in Tobias

By Lizette Strait

Every once in a while the stars and planets align just right, and things happen. I'm not talking about odd occurrences that if you look deep enough, there's an explanation. What I'm talking about is an event that leaves you speechless. Don't believe me? Well, let me tell you a story and you decide.

It was a warm summer evening in Tobias, and all was right in the world, and not. The heat and humidity had a grip on the town and people were edgy. The witch in me should've seen something was brewing but I didn't. Not sure why. Cooper women had the knack to foresee certain things. It was what we did.

My best friend Bev was hosting a party for the new police chief, Ares Stoner and I was late. Nothing unusual there. I promised to come early and help, but time got away from me. As I squeezed my lime green Nissan Cube between a pickup truck and a classic Cadillac convertible, my friend was on the porch waving for me to hurry up. I walked past the big yellow fins on the Cadillac and smiled. The Cinderella sisters were at the party.

Alma and Alvaretta Tobias were affectionately known as the Cinderella sisters. The two octogenarians were the last members of the town's founding family. Every day the ladies dressed in their finery and cruised around town searching for Prince Charming. Some hinted the reason neither sister married was because of lost loves. I doubted that theory. The two were uncatchable, though I imagine many had tried.

With my tiramisu cheesecake in hand, I

hurried up the sidewalk. I loved Bev's little bungalow. She had recently painted it brown and green with a bit of red. There were pink rose bushes lining the front of the house and wind chimes danced on the light breeze.

"You're late, Iris," Bev said.

"It wouldn't be me if I wasn't," I responded with a grin.

Bev grunted. It was her usual response when she was agitated.

"Do you want to hear why? Or will you continue to grumble?"

Bev wasn't mad. She just didn't handle parties well. Why she threw these things was beyond me.

"Come on inside and give me a hand. You can tell me all about it while you help," Bev said.

Low murmuring and soft music drifted through the little bungalow. Everyone was there, and the subdued group was going to live up to my expectations - boring.

"Do I have a story to tell you. You won't believe who I met on the way here," I said as I closed the front door behind me.

Bev examined the piece of paper I handed

her. "You got a ticket?"

"Yes, and I'll give you three guesses who gave it to me, but the first two don't count. And by the way, Bev, the new chief is a hunk," I said laced with sarcasm.

"Well, Ares isn't here yet and don't get your knickers in a knot about this. It'll work itself out."

Quiet laughter tickled my chest as I thought about the whole ticket episode. Was I laughing at myself because I wasn't paying attention to my driving? Or was it because of his swagger? Honestly, I didn't know.

As we headed toward the kitchen, I nodded to friends. All the town gossips were there and I wanted to linger. Not that I retold what I heard, I liked to know who was sleeping with whom but Bev pulled me along.

The kitchen was in complete chaos. Dishes and plates of food were everywhere. Potato and macaroni salads were competing for space on a chair. The table was piled high with desserts, and there was something boiling over on the stove.

"Take the lasagna out of the oven," my friend said, as she poured two glasses of Pinot Noir. Bev drained her glass, then refilled it and sipped again.

I searched for the potholders, and they were nowhere in sight, probably buried somewhere under the mounds of bags and boxes on the counter. I resorted on using a towel and got the pan out of the oven. Sweat beaded on my forehead. The wine soothed some of my discomfort.

"I'll start bringing the food out to the dining room," Bev said, standing in front of the swinging door. She balanced three covered dishes in her arms and held napkins in her hand. "Start the coffee."

"Sure, go ahead. I got it."

The door swung closed and my thoughts turned to making coffee. Someone grabbed me from behind, turned me around, and kissed my cheek.

"Iris," the man said with a bit of cheer in his voice.

"Rick, where did you come from?" I asked. He startled me and if it wasn't for my quick thinking, I would've dropped the carafe of water.

He smiled and wiggled his brows, "So I surprised you. I didn't think anyone could do that."

"I'm not all-seeing, Rick," I said with a chuckle.

I liked Rick and was happy my friend finally found someone who adored her. He was a nice guy, a gentleman, and treated Bev like a princess. And if truth be told, I had a hand in the two getting together. Bev had her sights set on Rick and she couldn't get him to ask her out. My friend begged me to brew a love potion and at first, I resisted. I never interfered in other people's lives. But Bev persisted and I gave in. Thank God it worked out.

"I got to get more ice. Hey, Bev told me you were bringing your special cake. She's tried to make it but it just isn't the same," Rick said as he opened the freezer.

"I did, but you have to be careful. I baked a file in it just in case I have to break out of jail."

Rick gave me a questioning look.

"I'll tell you later, Rick," Bev said as she came back into the kitchen.

"Oh, by the way, Ares called and said he's on his way. He had to drop off the cruiser, so he'll be here soon," Rick said.

"Oh, goodie, goodie," I muttered under my breath.

Bev and I headed into the living room to greet the new police chief. I wanted to have fun tonight and maybe just a bit of revenge. Okay, so I wasn't quite over the ticket incident.

"Looks like Bev's about to fling her girlfriend into your path," Rick said to Ares.

I hesitated in mid-step. Bev's campaign to fix me up with a man was just short of advertising on a billboard. Most times I took it in stride, but to be thrown in this man's path rubbed me the wrong way.

"Ares, you made it," Bev said.

"Yes, sorry for being late. I had some things to tie up before I could leave work." Ares' gaze strayed to me and his brows quirked up.

I shrugged and my chin lifted.

"Thank you for having me tonight. The party was very thoughtful. I brought you something," Ares continued. He handed a bottle of Pinot Noir to Bev. "It's an excellent year. I was surprised a liquor store in Tobias had it."

"We may be in the wilds of upstate New York, but we do like our hooch, Ares," Bev joked. "You should try the corn soup sometime. It's quite tasty."

"Corn soup?"

Bev ignored Ares' question about the local moonshine and examined the bottle of wine. "Iris, this is your favorite, isn't it?" Bev said showing the label to me.

Before I had a chance to agree, someone stumbled into me from behind, and I pitched forward. Strong hands reached out, and I found myself staring at a broad chest that tested the seams of the shirt that covered it. When I was released, I stepped back. I wanted to say something, my mouth opened but no words came out.

"Ares, this is Iris Cooper," Bev said, with a little bit too much cheek in her voice.

It was odd how the best-laid plans fall to pieces in a blink of an eye. How was I going to rib the man for pulling me over and giving me a ticket after falling into his arms?

"Hello, It's nice to see you again," I squeaked.

Ares tilted his head slightly to the left, lifted a brow, and flashed his pearly whites. "It's nice to be formally introduced to you, Ms. Cooper." He bowed slightly, his eyes never straying from mine.

"Did I miss something?"

"Rick, Ares pulled Iris over tonight on her way here. He gave her a ticket," Bev said.

"Really? What was her infraction? Speeding?" Rick lifted his beer to his lips hiding his smile.

"I don't speed. I'm just always running late," I retorted.

Wait. Why did I need to defend myself? I got a ticket for a broken blinker, not speeding. "Bev, the food is getting cold, and people are hungry," I said changing the subject.

"Yes, of course. Let's eat," my friend said.

Partygoers descended on the food like locusts. That's one thing about the people of Tobias. If there was food, they would come. I managed to find a plate and fill it with leftovers. Boy was it hot. Even with the air conditioning on full blast, I had to fan myself with my napkin. Maybe another glass of wine would help.

"There you are Iris," Bev said.

"I've been right here all along. What's wrong?" I asked.

Bev attacked the cluttered sideboard and started to straighten up the silverware. "That Lisa is really something. Her skirt couldn't get any shorter, could it?"

"Bait," I said with a smirk.

"Exactly," Bev said.

"Why did you invite her? Is she throwing a wrench into your plans of fixing me up with someone?" I asked.

From my vantage point, Lisa was standing next to Ares in the living room and hanging onto every word he was saying. I couldn't hear the conversation over the din, but it had to be quite interesting.

"I didn't invite her. She just showed up," Bev said.

I laughed. Ares and the brunette bombshell looked cute together. Too cute. My eyes narrowed.

"Hey, is there any more punch?" Rick asked, standing next to the dining room table. He scraped the bottom of the punch bowl with the ladle and poured the last of the red liquid in a cup.

"Yes. Can you refill it? I need to finish cleaning up the dining room. The fixings are on the buffet," Bev said.

"Sure," Rick said.

I was surprised the party was turning out to

be enjoyable. Good food. Good wine. Good company, if you excluded the new police chief. So he gave me a ticket. No big deal. It wasn't as if I never received one before. I sifted through the reasons why the man bothered me and always came to the same conclusion - I was attracted to him. Ridiculous.

No matter where my gaze landed, he was in my sights. I downed the last of my wine and dismissed my absurd thoughts about the new chief. A reconnaissance for dirty dishes was needed instead of me standing there with puppy eyes. I perused the living room and found two plates in the rubber tree plant pot.

"Hi Joan, are you done with your plate?" I asked. Joan nodded as she handed me her dish.

I lingered to listen to Joan and Lisa's conversation and amusement crossed my face. Obviously, Ares moved on and much to the brunette bombshell's dismay, left her behind. The only way to describe the two women was an Abbot and Costello duo. Not that they looked like the vaudeville comedy team, but it was the way they interacted with each other. Lisa, the statuesque brunette with her dry humor, played Joan, the short and well-endowed redhead well. But every once in a while Joan got the last word in.

"I'd love to get his number," Joan whispered, leaning closer to Lisa.

"Whose?" Lisa asked absently.

"Ares Stoner. Honestly, Lisa, I don't think you heard a word I said in the past five minutes."

Lisa shrugged. "Well, let's see who gets it first," she retorted.

I decided to have some fun with the two girls. They were always in competition for a man and not that I played favorites, I always rooted for Joan.

"I have it ladies, and I'll be happy to pass it along to you," I said.

The two girls stared at me with wide eyes. "You do?" Joan asked.

"Oh, yes, I have his number."

"And how did you get it. No, wait a minute. I bet Rick gave it to you. Totally an unfair advantage," Lisa said.

"I have no need for it, so I'll be happy to share it," I said.

"Well?" Lisa said impatiently.

"Nine-one-one."

Back in the kitchen, I helped Bev load the last of the plates into the dishwasher. It was an endless job but with the two of us working as a team, it went quickly. I grabbed the bottle of Pinot Noir off the counter and filled our glasses.

"Come in, Rick and Ares," I said with my back to the dining room door.

The swinging door opened a bit and Rick's smile peeked through. "See, I told you, she's a witch," he whispered to Ares.

"Yes, gentlemen, come in. I'm casting a spell to turn you two into toads."

Rick croaked loudly and pushed the door wide open. Bev and I laughed. "Be nice, Iris. We don't want to scare the new police chief away," Bev continued to chuckle.

The two men came into the kitchen. Rick had an idiot's grin on his face and wouldn't let the joke die. "Bev, kiss me. Ward off this enchantment and turn me back into Prince Charming," he said. Rick grabbed my friend around the waist, planted a big one on her lips, and then twirled her around.

Ares leaned against the counter and sipped his beer. His poker face gave nothing away and for some reason, I wanted to know what was running through his mind.

"Being a witch, you're not worried about being burned at the stake?" Ares asked.

Our eyes locked. "I enjoy being set on fire, but not at the stake." I lifted my wine to my lips, and with the tip of my tongue, I caught a drop of the red liquid running down the goblet.

Ares lifted his beer to his lips and tilted the bottle in my direction. "Touché."

Shouts and music reverberated through the walls causing the cabinet doors to vibrate. The kitchen floor rumbled with the beat of the dancing in the dining room.

"Come on, you fool. Let's find out what has everyone so rowdy," Bev said as she grabbed Rick's arm.

Ares started to get the message. Winking at him and giving the occasional well-placed jab was fun. Maybe getting the traffic ticket had some redeeming qualities.

In the dining room, a few partygoers were

jumping up and down to the beat of the song. Others were gathered around the table refilling their punch glasses. Bev disappeared into the crowd after she handed me a mug of coffee and asked me to give it to Ares. Glass crashed to the floor and everyone cheered. It was definitely time for coffee and I was glad I used the big coffee maker.

After picking up the broken punch cup, I went looking for Ares. He was standing in front of the rubber tree plant and I was surprised he was alone. "Are you having a good time?" He nodded, though I wasn't sure he heard what I said.

"Here, have some coffee." I handed him the mug.

Ares sipped the dark and bitter brew and winced.

"Don't you like it?"

Ares sipped again. "It's fine. It just has an unusual aftertaste."

"I can get you some cream and sugar if it will help."

"No, that's okay." He lifted the mug and took another sip. "I like my coffee black, and it's starting to taste pretty good."

"Good." I smiled. Maybe he wasn't that bad after all, but still, Greek gods are not my type. "If you'll excuse me, I have to get more coffee. The music was at a lull and I could actually hear myself think.

"Iris?" Ares asked. His low baritone voice stopped me in mid-step.

"Yes, Ares? Is there something you want?"

"To set you on fire."

"The guy is a nut," I said.

"Who are you talking about?" Bev asked.

"Ares Stoner." I continued to stare at the police chief over Bev's shoulder. His gaze never faltered from mine even when he sipped his coffee.

Ok, Ares' misunderstanding was my fault. I should've never teased him in the kitchen, but for his demeanor to change so quickly was odd.

"Why do you say that?" Bev's question had a little bit too much merriment to it, which raised my suspicion.

I pulled my focus from Ares and directed all my attention on my friend. "What do you know about this, Bev?"

"Nothing. Why don't you go ask him for a date? I think he likes you."

After giving Bev a disbelieving once over, I looked at the nut again drinking his coffee. "You know something."

Bev shrugged. "It's a full moon tonight. Maybe the lunar gravitational pull affects him more than others."

Howling echoed outside and the partygoers responded to the call of the wild. My eyes widened when Rosanne, the owner of the local yarn shop, Clicking Sticks, bellowed out her lungs. I didn't know her well, but she always spoke in hush tones and knitted for a living.

A crash split the moment. A TV tray laid on its side, broken plates and glasses scattered across the floor.

"Mayor Jensen, leave the lampshade alone please," Bev yelled over to the short stocky man. "I'll be right back," she said and darted across the room.

I looked over at Ares again, and he licked his lips. The man licked his lips! Maybe it was the full moon. What other explanation could there be for his change in behavior?

Ares advanced. His panther-like steps were precise, his jaw set. I decided escape would be my best option, but I didn't make it. Muscular arms grabbed me from behind and twirled me around. His blue eyes sparkled with mischief and a shade of seduction. I was good and caught.

"Chief Stoner, please release me," I said with as much authority I could muster.

"Am I forgiven?" Ares whispered in my ear.

"For what?"

"For giving you a ticket."

"Yes, yes, of course, you are. Now let me go."

"Never. I'm going to set you ablaze." His warm breath heated my neck, and a cacophony of conflicting feelings swamped me.

Sirens blared. My God, the police are coming. But how could they? Practically the entire force was there. Disturbed's 'Indestructible' poured out the stereo's speakers, and I sighed. Someone had changed the radio station and turned the volume to the max.

But my relief didn't last long. Alvaretta Tobias climbed onto a dining room chair and began to sing along with the song. The group surrounding her cheered as she shimmied and shook her shoulders. My God, this was not good. The eighty-plus-year-old woman could fall and break a hip.

"Ares, you got to let me go. I got to get Alvaretta down from that chair," I said, my voice almost desperate.

"Your mine. Rick can get her down."

Frustration didn't begin to explain what I felt. No matter how many times I pried a hand from me, another one replaced it to stake a claim.

"Ares, if you let me go, I'll be right back. I'll go get a match and we can burn together," I said.

After a few moments, he agreed. I didn't think it would actually work, but it did. Ares released his hold and I nearly fell to the floor.

"I'll be right back."

"Hurry," Ares said with a wink.

With one crisis on hold, I rushed over to Alvaretta. The ring of partygoers surrounding the singing octogenarian was tough to push through, so I looked for Bev to help. I scanned the dining room and my eyes widened. Duncan had Alvaretta's sister Alma Tobias cornered against the china closet. Did Duncan just pinch her butt? I blinked to clear my vision. Yup, he did.

"I love you, Alma. Run away with me and we'll make passionate love together," Duncan said in a fake French accent.

I had known Duncan all of my life. He was always an unassuming man who didn't have much to say, until now.

Pandemonium. That was the only way the night could be described. Somehow I had walked into someone's drug-induced flashback, and I couldn't find the exit. I needed answers on how the party steamrolled into chaos and Bev had the answer. Where was she? She knew something and I was going to get it out of her.

"There you are, Bev. Help me get Alvaretta down from that chair," I said. Bev had come out of the kitchen. We broke through Alvaretta's fans and eased her to the floor.

"Thank you ladies, but it wasn't necessary," Alvaretta said. She smiled, straightened the pearls around her neck and turned away.

It didn't take long for Alvaretta to continue her mischief. She was chasing Bill the barber and the two disappeared into the kitchen.

Bedlam continued to build. The walls of the small bungalow shook as 'Piece of My Heart', blasted out of the stereo speakers. I could barely hear myself think. Mayor Jensen and his wife, Sylvia, had lampshades on their heads, and Rosanne, the knitter, was chasing a young patrol officer around the dining room table.

I caught up to Bev in the living room. She was picking up discarded napkins and turned down the radio.

"Bev, I think it's time to end the party," I said. I picked up a full punch cup that was on the edge of the coffee table.

"Yes, of course. I don't have a clue why everyone is acting this way."

"You don't?" I asked.

"No."

I looked over at Ares standing next to the rubber tree plant. Ares was ready to pounce. His sultry stare was getting hotter by the minute. He walked over and asked, "Did you get the match?"

"Match?" Bev asked.

"Yes, he wants to set me on fire, Bev," I replied.

Ares took a sip of his coffee and Bev blanched.

"Ok, what's going on? It's obvious you know something," I said.

"Well, I can explain him," Bev hooked a thumb in Ares' direction, "but not all of this." Her eyes surveyed the chaotic party. "I sort of put some of your leftover love potion in Ares' mug.

"What?!" I stared at Ares, and without thinking, downed the red liquid in the punch cup.

"Great party," Rick said. He had come in from the dining room holding an empty bottle. "Is there any more of this Jamaican rum? The punch bowl is empty again and everyone is thirsty."

Bev paled. A red flush crept up her neck and she wiped beads of sweat from her forehead with a napkin. "Rick, tell me you didn't use that in the punch." Bev pointed to the empty bottle in his hand.

"Yes, it gives the punch a good kick."

"That's the bottle that held your love potion," Bev said to me. "But I swear I only used a few drops for Ares' coffee. The bottle was practically full when I put it back on the buffet."

The realization of what was causing the

pandemonium swept over me, then I looked at the empty punch cup in my hand. My focus turned to Ares and a seductive smile settled on my lips. I put the cup down, removed the mug from Ares' grip and swallowed the last of the coffee.

Grabbing Ares' hand, I dragged him behind me. "Come on, I know where there's a box of matches."

When I look back at that summer's night of lunacy, I laugh. For the first time, I got to see what people were like under their facades. Some of the townsfolk have inhibitions that were buried so deep, their spontaneity never see the light of day.

I'm not sure if anyone remembers what had happened at the party. If they do, no one mentions it. But I have a feeling there are some lingering effects. Not that I repeat gossip, but I hear a patrol car has been seen parked behind 'Clicking Sticks' after the yarn shop is closed. And last weekend, Alma Tobias went to Lake Placid for a few days with a man who has yet to be named. Titillating.

Sheriff Stoner has settled into Tobias, and

every time I see him, his gaze turns sultry, making my heart flutter. I'm still trying to figure this out. Maybe I'll bring Ares a rubber tree plant for his office since I hear he has gained an affinity for the potted plant.

I feel guilty about what happened and should never have agreed to brew the concoction for Bev. What the hell was I thinking? At the time, I believed Rick needed a push to ask Bev out, and their natural chemistry would take over. Was I wrong?

No, of course, I wasn't. The potion wasn't a true love potion. I'm not a bona fide witch and don't know any hocus pocus. It was a tincture of herbs with no magical powers. There had to be other forces influencing the madness at the party.

Maybe it was the combination of the full moon and celestial bodies aligning. Venus was rising toward Orion, and if you looked up into the sky, it appeared the Mighty Hunter was calling the Goddess of Love to him. Add this to the hypnotic moon frequency, everyone released their inhibitions and had a hell of a time.

A Summer's Night in Tobias

SPECIAL

THANKS

TO OUR

KICKSTARTER

BACKERS

Catey C.

Mrs. Hudson

Geoff & Dawn Harvey

Melissa & Matt

Natalie Werner

Mary Beth Frezon

Mark Lee

Stephanie Nolan

KarenMarie Kauderer

Irene Adler

Herb Kauderer

Wilson & Elsie Movic

Shan Jeniah Burton

Elizabeth A. Janes

Betsy & Bora Gumustop

Andy Lee

Shane Alonso

Anthiem

Wompa

Susan Blackley

Han Marshall

Mitchell Karlick

Bobbi Boyd

Hisa Futaba

Kevin Kuhne

Sharyn Kolberg

Dr. James Watson

Beckey Carlson-Lee

Maria Cloos

Jaimie Miller

Mary Lee

Marilyn Nugent

Evelyn Kauderer

Debra Brenner

The Biles Family

Shannon Grant

Jaz Johnson

Mary Beth Buchner

Sam T Willis

Sherlock Holmes

Liz Wyatt

Leslie D'Angona

Rosemary Blodgett